ORION'S BELT

ORION'S BELT

BALMUIR
BOOK
PUBLISHING
LTD.

JOHN STARNES

ISBN 0-919511-16-3 (paper)
ISBN 0-919511-17-1 (cloth)

Cover illustration by Jay R. Freeborn

For my sons and friends,
Colin John Starnes and
Patrick Barclay Starnes.

Orion's Belt
is the third book in a trilogy of novels by John
Starnes. The previously published titles in the set
are *Deep Sleepers* and *Scarab*. The three
novels are also available together in a boxed set
under the title:
The Dissemblers
a trilogy of Canadian spy stories

Prologue

Brad Randall, Director General of the RCMP Security Service, recalled vividly the 3 a.m. telephone call from George McCain, informing him that a Czech national calling himself Jan Rudiczech, a passenger on a Cuban Airlines flight from Prague to Havana, was seeking political asylum at Gander airport.

In itself, a defection at Gander was not extraordinary. Scores of travellers from the Soviet bloc had sought and received asylum in Canada since Cuban Airlines acquired landing rights there years earlier. But this particular request was unusual. Jan Rudiczech was no ordinary defector. He came bearing a mysterious and unusual gift, addressed to Brad Randall.

The gift, a *cloisonné* oval in various shades of blue, the size of a seagull's egg, turned out to be an exquisite example of the art of Peter Carl Gustavovich Fabergé, the Russian goldsmith, renowned for the fine gold-encrusted enamelware he made in St. Petersburg in the late 19th and early 20th centuries. Brad recognized it, having seen similar examples of Fabergé's work in museums in New York and Berlin. Skilfully hinged, it contained a small piece of paper with the typed words, "Paul and Patricia with love". Brad immediately knew, which was obviously the author's intention, that the gift was intended for Paul Gribanov. Paul was the only son of KGB Colonel Galena Nadya Gribanov who, a few years earlier, Brad had identified as a Soviet spy in the Privy Council Office. Under the name of Mrs. Heide Latour, one of a string of aliases she had used since her recruitment during the second world war and her training at the old NKVD espionage school near Moscow, she had penetrated the Canadian foreign service and Cabinet office. Brad had "doubled" her and, under the code name "Opal", she provided the RCMP Security Service and friendly foreign intelligence services with much valuable information.

He also remembered with chagrin the day she gave him the slip and returned to Russia with her son Paul. An exhaustive review of the case failed to establish exactly what went wrong. It was generally accepted that her initial co-operation with the Security Service was genuine. She believed that the NKVD had murdered her father on Stalin's orders. Her decision to return to the Soviet Union came only after her discovery, through a surreptitious wireless contact with Moscow Centre, that her father was, in fact, alive and on a mission to Canada.

Galena Nadya Gribanov was a worthy adversary. Brad had developed more than professional respect and admiration for her. There was an affection bordering on love, or at least infatuation, that was rekindled whenever, in the succeeding years, his work brought reminders of her.

Jan Rudiczech's arrival in Gander bearing the Fabergé egg had been one such reminder. Another had been the drama surrounding the return of her son, Paul, to Canada. Now under the protection of the Security Service, Paul had been instrumental in thwarting a terrorist attempt to blow up the Welland Canal. The ship carrying the terrorists, the MS *Nefertiti*, was sunk in the Gulf of St. Lawrence. According to the news media there were no survivors. In fact Paul Gribanov had already left the vessel, but his escape was kept secret in an effort to protect him from retaliation by the KGB.

The Patricia referred to in the note was Patricia Ballantyne, who had gone to Leningrad as an exchange student. There she and Paul had met and loved. After Paul's return to Canada the two had married and, courtesy of the Security Service, been provided with completely new identities and the financial help needed to launch a new life in a small, tranquil town in southern Ontario. Jan Rudiczech's defection and the message in the Fabergé egg ended the tranquility. Obviously Galena Nadya was aware that Paul was alive. Probably others in the KGB knew, too. Brad immediately ordered a complete change of identity for them. Further, since he could not exclude the possibility that the source of the information about Paul's survival and marriage was a leak within the Security Service, he confined knowledge of their new identity and location to three of his closest colleagues.

The disruption was not easy for the newlyweds. Patricia was shaken at having to abandon the small house with only a few hours notice. She had put so much effort into making it distinctively her own. The small garden, the furnishings, the colours, the materials all bore her imprint. Everything was left behind. They took only the clothes and personal items they could pack into a few suitcases. Three days later, all traces of their former identities were erased — they no longer existed.

With new identities, they were resurrected in Halifax. Bankrolled by the Security Service through a dummy parent company with its head office in Toronto, Cancom Inc., Paul was set up as the owner of a small TV and radio rental repair business on Barrington Street. The business was registered in Paul's new name. A joint bank account with $50,000 was opened for the couple in a nearby branch of the Bank of Nova Scotia and they were able to move at once into a furnished 6th floor apartment in a building on Spring Garden Road. For the early part of their re-settlement, they were kept under discreet protective surveillance — extensive enough, however, for Brad to be one of the first people to know when Patricia became pregnant.

Rudiczech proved to be a cool customer, asking for proof of Brad's identity before agreeing to talk or hand over the Fabergé egg. He claimed to have no idea who might have given it to him. According to him, he found it on the floor of his Moscow apartment when he returned from work one day, a piece of paper affixed to the brown wrapper with Brad Randall's name and the initials "RCMP".

"In my business, your name was well known to me. I was unlikely to forget it. We both know it would have been dangerous to keep the label. I destroyed it and hid the egg with its message."

Rudiczech claimed the incident had scared him since it meant someone suspected he was planning to defect, a secret he said he had shared with nobody. He postponed his plans. When no further incident occurred in the weeks that followed he revitalized them and proceeded with his defection. Although sceptical of his story, the Security Service accepted the explanation provisionally, particularly after they confirmed his identity. He was Colonel Igor Petr Molodny. Known to Western intelligence and security services as "Orion", he was the KGB co-ordinator of various East bloc intelligence services. His possession of the Fabergé egg helped establish his credentials. Paul Gribanov was able to confirm that the Fabergé piece was a family heirloom, although he was not able to tell them much more than that.

Orion's defection caused a stir in the Ottawa intelligence community. He was quite a catch. Friendly, and some not so friendly, foreign agencies would be beating a path to Brad's door. Among the reasons Orion gave for wishing to defect to Canada was the fact that the country possessed some of the world's most highly renowned plastic surgeons. He explained that in order to avoid assassination, he wished to change his appearance. Given the extent of the knowledge he possessed about past and present KGB operations and assets in place in North America and Britain, he claimed that when his defection became known, orders for his liquidation would be issued immediately. He claimed there was urgency to the matter since he knew of three agents in Canada who probably would be able to identify him, but whose identity he did not know. All he did know was that they were in the employ of the Canadian government, perhaps even in the RCMP Security Service!

That he was code-named "Orion", the giant hunter of Greek mythology noted for his beauty, was apposite. Although no giant, Molodny was six feet tall and well built. His Grecian profile, reddish-blonde hair and striking, dark brown eyes seldom went unnoticed by either sex. As an added precaution, Brad turned to the British and the Americans to seek confirmation of his identity. There were CIA and British SIS agents who knew Molodny. One CIA agent had actually worked with him in Bucharest. An SIS agent had sought to lure him to bed with her in an unsuccessful honey trap operation. Both agents were flown to Ottawa. From a special room fitted with one-way glass and a means of hearing his responses, they observed Molodny under interrogation. The American was quite positive.

"That's the son of a bitch. Good looking and knows it. Sharp dresser, with an eye for the ladies. Don't be fooled by his appearance. He's a cold, calculating bastard who would gladly crucify his mother if he thought it would be to his advantage. If his defection *is* genuine, there has to be something in it for him. I'd watch him like a hawk."

The British agent smiled at her colleague's response.

"Yes, that's him. I wonder if he likes honey with his tea."

One

Marianne Carrière looked down from the window of her eleventh floor apartment. She saw the official blue sedan waiting on the circular driveway below. In it were two men, one in RCMP uniform.

"The car's here, Brad."

The muffled reply reached her from the bathroom.

"Thanks. I'll be out in a minute. How about another cup of coffee?"

Emerging from the bathroom, Brad joined Marianne at the small table by the wide window overlooking the Ottawa River and the Gatineau hills beyond. Here they often enjoyed both breakfast and the view. The bright red braces, which he had bought during his last trip to London were set off to advantage against the plain white shirt he was wearing. His penchant for colourful braces had long since been accepted by his RCMP colleagues as an idiosyncrasy to be tolerated.

Marianne watched as he sipped his coffee. He was a good looking man who had weathered well. He kept himself in condition without making a fetish of it. His wavy, black hair was flecked with grey. Around the temples it had turned white. Distinguished, she thought. The laugh lines around his eyes were deeply etched, accentuating his aquiline nose. His eyes, though, were the feature she liked best. Brown flecked with green, they were barometers of his mood. They could change rapidly from laughter to anger, from trust to suspicion. At the moment they were neutral. They had been fortunate in the relationship which had built up between them over the years. Both divorced — never re-married — it suited them equally. They were comfortable with the arrangement, entailing as it did no third parties, no children, no binding commitments other than those provided by common law.

"Good coffee."

"It's the last of the Blue Mountain you brought back from Jamaica."

"Not much chance of my getting more for a while. Which reminds me, I'll probably be away for the next few days. I should know later today. The suitcase I need is at my apartment, so I'll leave from there."

Finishing his coffee, Brad rose from the table and slipped on the jacket he had left lying on the sofa. He was conscious of the added weight of the 9mm Kaba Special automatic resting in the zippered pocket, built into the inner left side of the jacket by the regimental tailor. The weapon had been modified by the RCMP armourer, fitted with a special safety catch which could be easily manipulated by the thumb of the right hand as the pistol was withdrawn from its concealed cloth holster. While not accurate beyond ten feet, the small Belgian-manufactured gun with a clip of five bullets was deadly. It was perfectly adequate for its purpose — Brad's protection. He had protested when it was first suggested that he carry a sidearm. His officers had remained adamant. They argued that there were times when even the constant and extensive coverage of Level IV protection might not be able to preserve his life. At first, not having carried a weapon for years, he felt self-conscious and somewhat silly. Now, he seldom noticed. He had to admit that there had been one or two occasions in the past few weeks when he had been reassured to know the gun was there.

Leaning over Marianne, he kissed her lightly on the forehead.

"Bye, love. Take care. I'll phone you later at your office to let you know my plans."

She pulled him toward her.

"Brad Randall. That's no way to say goodbye. Give me a real kiss."

He lifted her to her feet as he did so. In her slippers, she was a full ten inches shorter than he. Brad felt her warmth through the thin negligée, running his hands down the exciting outline of her body. He also felt the hardness of his own response, something she could always arouse in him. He broke away, laughing.

"Any more of that and I'll book off sick."

As Brad emerged from the apartment building, he was greeted by the two men at the car. The uniformed driver saluted smartly and opened the rear door for him.

"Morning, Stan. Morning, Corporal McCrea."

As the car pulled away from the curb, the Director General of the RCMP Security Service leaned back on the cushions of the rear seat. He was able to see the driver in the rear-view mirror. The face that confronted him was not a handsome one. His black eyebrows were too heavy, his left ear a cauliflower. The crooked nose looked like the result of a failed professional boxing career. Given the man's physique, it seemed quite likely. The light blue eyes might have denoted a background to match his Scot's name. Brad Randall was among the few who knew that this was not the case. Stanley

Hydchuck, sitting watchfully beside Corporal McCrea in the front seat was another who knew.

"This is an unexpected pleasure, Stan."

"I didn't think you would mind. We had an early appointment with the plastic surgeon in the west end, so I thought we might as well pick you up en route rather than send another car. Besides, I knew you would want to see Igor for yourself. The doctors are pleased with his progress."

The driver looked into the mirror and gave a crooked smile, a gesture of friendliness belied by the unyielding expression in the eyes.

"How are things going, Igor?"

"Everything seems fine. As Mr. Welch says, the doctors seem pleased with my condition."

Brad had to keep reminding himself that Sergeant Stanley Hydchuck was only known to Igor Petr Molodny, alias Jan Rudiczech, alias RCMP Corporal Angus McCrea, as Stan Welch. Brad shifted slightly to obtain a better view of the driver's face. It was a high tribute to the professional skills of the plastic surgeons who had changed the handsome features of the former KGB Colonel to those of Angus McCrea.

Brad's car pulled into the inner courtyard at RCMP headquarters. The driver parked it carefully in the reserved space marked "Director General". With Stan Hydchuck leading the way, they entered by a rear door into which had been set two specially constructed dead-bolt locks. On the fourth floor George McCain met them at the steel-grille.

"Morning, Sir. If you have a moment, there are a couple of things we might discuss."

"Fine. On this floor?"

"Briefing room."

Stanley Hydchuck led Orion off down the long corridor. Brad Randall and McCain followed, stopping at an unmarked door. A digital lock was affixed to the steel frame. George McCain pushed a series of numbers. The heavy metal door swung inwards on well-oiled hinges, admitting them to a large, well-lit room. To one side, facing an empty wall space stood a long, semi-circular table behind which were a half dozen swivel chairs, upholstered in simulated black leather. Before each chair was a small table microphone, a couple of control buttons, and a grey telephone. At each place was a writing tablet and a couple of the ubiquitous yellow lead pencils with "Government of Canada" stamped on them in gold lettering. Brad wondered idly if the Auditor General had ever calculated how many taxpayers' dollars had been lost over the years through pilferage. Taken over the decade, Brad reckoned the figure might even run into the millions.

They settled into adjacent chairs. McCain pushed one of the buttons in front of him. It lit, indicating the microphone was active.

"Okay, ready when you are."

The lights dimmed and a screen lowered silently into place on the wall opposite them. The narrator's voice, which Brad recognized as that of John Merrivale, Head of the Special Analysis Group, burst from the overhead speakers.

"This morning's briefing is the result of our overnight analysis of yesterday's interrogation of Orion and earlier material. We have attempted to reduce our findings to a small number of charts which will appear in the form of coloured slides. I will comment as we proceed."

Brad leaned forward and activated his microphone.

"Before you begin, John. Have we any confirmation from London yet on the leads we provided them with?"

"No. There was no overnight traffic from London on the case. However, as you know, the leads we gave the Americans appear more promising. We intend to cover this aspect during the briefing."

"I have read the messages from Washington. Okay, go ahead."

The briefing lasted forty-eight minutes. Brad and McCain reserved their questions and comments until it was finished. When the lights were turned on, Merrivale joined them at the table.

"Thanks, John. That was comprehensive. The slides were helpful. In essence, however, thirty-one days of intense interrogation and twice as many days of surveillance have given us a detailed picture of Molodny's early life, training and career but precious little to satisfy us that his defection is genuine. True, he has pointed us in the direction of persons who could be the three spies he claims exist in the government. However, he has produced nothing sufficiently convincing to warrant seeking Ministerial authority for the kind of intrusive investigation which probably would be necessary to confirm such suspicions as we might entertain. The most promising lead he has given us suggests a political figure — precisely the area Ministers will regard as too sensitive to consider without an ironclad case. To obtain Ministerial agreement to investigate political figures or members of their staffs will take a hell of a lot more than he has given us to date."

Merrivale took off his glasses and cleaned them with his handkerchief.

"What you say is true. Nothing Orion has provided to us about Canadians can be corroborated — at least not at this time. We are left with the possibility that the information we passed to the Americans will be corroborated, although its current market value still has to be determined. The most convincing thing he has done so far is to have voluntarily submitted to facial surgery. That would have been an ordeal for anyone. In his case, the extraordinarily ugly transformation must have been traumatic. He is extremely vain. Only some strong motive such as fear of assassination or ideological fanaticism could have caused him to go through with it."

George McCain grunted.

"Merrivale may be right, but I don't trust the bastard. Never have. He's holding back. I think he's a phoney."

Brad intervened.

"Of course he's holding back, George. Have you ever known a defector who didn't? Remember Galena Gribanov? It took weeks of prodding to get much out of her."

"Yeah, and look what happened in the end. She made fools of us."

"Okay, okay. We don't need to be reminded of that aspect of the case."

"You were the one who brought it up. I'll agree that Orion's face-lift is pretty convincing, but it's going to take a whole lot more to persuade me that he's on the level. We need much more out of him. The question is how to get it and quickly. Ministers are going to get cold feet unless we can come up with something concrete soon. They're already as nervous as cats that the story will leak. Just imagine what the Opposition will be able to make out of the fact that instead of clapping him in prison as an enemy spy, we are keeping him in the lap of luxury at RCMP headquarters."

The three of them fell silent contemplating the scenario described by George McCain, one not so far-fetched if historical precedent meant anything.

"Okay, I'll have to report to the Committee and to Ministers by Thursday. In the meantime, I plan a quick trip to Washington to see if I can find out more about the leads he has given the Americans."

* * * * * * * * * * * * * * * * * * *

With the help of a strong tail-wind, the RCMP Cessna got Brad to Dulles International airport by 2:30 that same afternoon. Unfortunately, Washington National airport, which was in the city, refused to allow small aircraft on unscheduled flights. He was met by Sam Colt, a junior member of Silas Yates' secretariat, and driven directly to CIA headquarters at Langley, Virginia. He was sitting in Silas' office by 3:30. Also present was Caspar J. Buller Jr., Silas' successor on the Agency's counter espionage desk, and Brad's old friend, Matt Villiers, who had recently taken over the Russian desk from Roger Vine. Brad and Villiers first met in Germany, years earlier, when Brad was a Visa Control officer with the Canadian

Immigration Office in Cologne. Villiers was then a member of the CIA station in Bonn. A couple of difficult cases brought them together, Villiers helped Brad with the Opal investigation and Brad, in turn, was able to pull the chestnuts out of the fire for Villiers in a case involving the use of a false Canadian passport by a Czech espionage agent operating in Berlin. Villiers' family was of French origin, the founder of the American branch being André de Villiers, a cavalry lieutenant in a regiment under General Lafayette's command. The "de" was dropped with time and the name, although spelled as it was in the 1700's, was now pronounced "Veelers", much to the annoyance of the French branch of the family. Matt had long since resigned himself to the American pronunciation of his ancient name.

Brad's CIA colleagues listened without comment while he filled them in on the results of Orion's interrogations.

"As you will appreciate, Orion hasn't told us anything which enables us to judge whether he is genuine. He's pointed us in directions which could be promising, but without a lot more investigative work, much of which would have to be intrusive, we are unlikely to get very far. It will take time — perhaps weeks."

Brad didn't want to explain that it was not so much time that worried him as it was the likelihood that the government, which was lukewarm about granting Orion political asylum in the first place, might seek to renege on the affair. He probably didn't need to be explicit. Caspar Buller was no fool and Silas had had enough dealings with Canadians to know the score. Brad continued.

"That leaves the leads which Orion has provided for you and the British. So far the British have failed to come up with anything. I gather your initial investigations have been a bit more encouraging?"

Silas cleared his throat.

"Depends what you mean by encouraging. At first blush it did seem that one of the leads might hit pay-dirt. However, further investigation has been disappointing. Seems we may have been too optimistic. We are continuing the investigation but, like you, we need more time — probably much more time."

Silas turned to his colleagues.

"Want to add anything?"

Both shook their heads. After a further half hour, during which Brad answered their questions about Orion, the meeting broke up. Villiers offered to escort Brad to the front door to sign him out.

"What now, Brad?"

"I guess I'll fly back to Ottawa tonight. The trip hasn't been very productive. I'm disappointed, although I don't know what I expected. I've an odd feeling about that meeting. Oh well, you win some, you lose some."

Matt gave him a strange look.

"Unless you particularly like flying in that Cessna at night, why don't you stay and get an early start tomorrow morning? Louise's cooking is as good as always and we'd be glad to put you up. How about it?"

Something in Villiers' voice and in his expression caught Brad's attention. Was he trying to suggest something? He had a hunch he was.

"That's very kind of you, Matt. Why not? I can think of nothing nicer. Are you sure it won't be an imposition?"

"Friends are never an imposition, Brad. Where would you like to go now?"

"I could usefully spend some time at the Embassy."

"Good. I'll have a car take you and I'll plan to pick you up there at about a quarter to six. Okay?"

"Fine."

Brad spent the intervening time talking to his liaison officers and in buying a large bunch of long-stemmed yellow roses. If his memory served him well, they were Louise's favourite. It was the perfect choice. Her pleasure bubbled over, enhanced by the fact that the following day was her birthday. She hugged him.

"Brad. What a darling you are. My favourite flowers from my favourite Canadian. Thank you. I am so glad you're here. We'll have a chance to talk. The last time I saw you was at that enormous party given by the Director at Chevy Chase. Impossible to hear a word and spooks everywhere. Spooks, that's all I ever get to talk to, spooks."

"Easy, Louise. Remember Brad is chief spook in Canada."

"Sorry, Brad. I don't count you as a spook — at least not the crashingly boring kind that Matt works with."

"Don't worry. I know what you mean. Besides, I hardly count myself as a spook of any kind — a spook-chaser, perhaps, and not a very good one at that. How are the boys?"

"They're fine, but they're hardly boys now — twenty-seven and thirty respectively."

Over drinks and during dinner, a delicious example of Louise's cooking skills, they continued to catch up on one another's lives. Brad was grateful that neither of them brought up the subject of Gwenneth, whom they had both known in Germany. Although divorced from her for many years, the memory still rankled. The failure, he now was able to acknowledge, had been as much his fault as it was hers. From references he made about Marianne, they would gather he was not without feminine influence in his life. He gave them high marks for not prying.

"Brad, I hope you will excuse me. I'm teaching at the Fletcher School and I have an early morning lecture to prepare. I'm sure that you and Matt have business to discuss. I'll say goodbye now since I'll probably be out before you leave in the morning."

After Louise left them, Matt offered Brad a liqueur.

"You still like Calvados? I have a half-bottle left of some marvellous stuff I picked up in Normandy a few months ago. We took a ten day holiday at a small village ten miles inland from the coast. If I ever leave this business, that's where I want to spend my summers."

When they were settled with balloon glasses of pale liquid gold, Matt turned to Brad.

"The Orion case is worrying you a lot?"

"Yes. I wasn't entirely frank this afternoon. If we don't get some concrete evidence soon that Orion is what he claims to be, I'm afraid the government will get cold feet and call the whole thing off. In that case, we will likely try to turn him over to your people or to the Brits. God knows what the others who know about him — the Swiss, the Germans, the Israelis and the Italians — will think. Our stock with them won't exactly soar. Of course, the government couldn't care less. In the present political climate all they care about is avoiding any situation which leaves them open to criticism from the opposition parties. If the story about Orion leaks out, they can envisage all too clearly the hue and cry that will follow. The Security Service will be accused of being soft on Communism. As usual, we would be unable to make an effective rebuttal."

"Well, you weren't the only one who wasn't being frank."

Brad leaned forward. His hunch had been right.

"What do you mean?"

"We've been friends for many years. I trust you but what I'm going to tell you will have to be handled with great care. My job would be on the line if Silas and the Director thought I'd spilled the beans. I must have a promise that the information I give you will not be communicated to your officials and Ministers."

"I appreciate what you're asking me, but the problem is that if the information has a bearing on whether the Canadian government is to continue the investigation, it isn't much use unless I can impart it to those who must take that decision."

"I thought as much, but unless I can have your promise that the information will not find its way back to Washington and implicate me, I can't give it to you."

Brad sat for a moment without speaking. He made a quick decision.

"Okay, Matt. Would you agree to let me inform the Prime

Minister and nobody else? It won't be the first time she has been made privy to information which could not be made available to anyone else in the government. I'd have to be able to explain the circumstances frankly, although I am sure that she would not want names. She could make up her mind on the basis of the information — whether to continue the case. If she's not satisfied and decides against further investigation — in other words to abandon Orion and have him 'placed' elsewhere — the knowledge you give me will remain with her and with me and nobody else. I will make sure that there are no written records of any kind."

"All right, Brad. Agreed, albeit reluctantly."

Villiers re-filled their glasses.

"When Silas Yates said that our investigation of Orion's leads was disappointing, he was seriously bending the truth. In fact one of those leads, involving a physical description, led us directly to a middle-grade official in the National Security Agency — a man with twelve years cypher-breaking experience, much of it in the counter-espionage field. We were lucky. When investigators picked him up for questioning, he was hungry — very hungry — for heroin."

"Heroin! Jesus."

"I know. You're wondering how such an obvious addiction could have escaped his annual security check-up. We don't know, but it did. Apparently for quite some time. It provided us with tremendous leverage. He broke almost immediately. A native born American of Lithuanian extraction from California, he was recruited in the early sixties."

"Through his addiction?"

"Ironically, no. However, it might well have been. It wouldn't be the first time the KGB have tried to use heroin to suborn one of our agents. There was the classic case a couple of years ago when the KGB, unknown to us, kidnapped one of our station chiefs in Europe — they administered knock-out drops and then injected him with heroin to induce addiction. Because he had a peculiar medical condition, the attempt failed."

"Charming."

"In the case of the NSA employee, the principal motivation appears to have been ideological. His heroin addiction has been a recent affair."

"Was he KGB?"

"Initial recruitment was by the Cubans acting as surrogates. The KGB took over as soon as he was hooked.

"Did they know he was on heroin?"

"The man, whom we have code-named "Firefly", claims they didn't, but his interrogators simply don't believe him. For one thing, he needed increasingly large sums of money to pay for his habit. He could only have received that kind of money from the

Mafia or the KGB. It must have been getting pricey even for the KGB."

"Why was Silas holding back?"

"Interrogation to date suggests he has done a great deal of damage. We don't know how much yet. Only time will tell."

Brad nodded his understanding, but Matt Villers continued.

"Firefly wasn't the only reason why Silas was being coy with you. From Firefly we learned that the CIA itself may have been penetrated at a very senior level. It hasn't been possible to pinpoint the person, but if it is whom we suspect, we're in trouble — deep trouble. The Agency needs time to continue what is a very tricky investigation. Certainly we're in no position to explain our suspicions to the 'Noforn' intelligence and security communities, even if we thought that wise."

Brad whistled softly.

"Boy, what a mess. I appreciate your having told me. As you know, our Prime Minister is a pretty tough lady. I will be surprised if she does not agree to allow us to continue our investigations, even if it involves political figures or persons close to them."

Matt got up and brought the nearly empty bottle of Calvados to where they were sitting.

"Some more? Looks as if you've got at least as many problems as we have."

"No thanks, Matt. I've had plenty. Besides, in Normandy I'm told it is considered bad luck for friends to drain a bottle of Calvados they've shared. Means they will quarrel."

"Well, we can't risk that, can we?"

Two

A light drizzle was falling by the time the Dulles International control tower gave the Cessna clearance to take off. Brad buckled himself into the seat in the cabin which he had to himself. He stared out of the small window idly wondering why the rivulets of rain appeared to defy gravity in the shifting, crazy pattern they made on the thick plastic. He was glad he was alone and didn't have to scream pleasantries above the noise of the engines. He welcomed the opportunity to think through the implications of what he had learned from Matt Villiers. It was quite a story. No wonder the Agency had been so close-mouthed. He would have to tread carefully if he was to avoid getting Matt in hot water. His mind went back to the early days of the Orion case.

* * * * * * * * * * * * * * * * * * * *

"The whole thing stinks to high heaven. He's as phoney as a cigar-store indian. I say we shouldn't touch it."

Tom Driver's stubby forefinger stabbed the air in the direction of Chief Superintendent Sandy Goodwin, sitting across the table from him.

"But, Tom, it's too early to be able to say that. Hell, the guy's only been here for a few hours. We haven't even got much beyond name, rank and serial number. If he is genuine, he could be a gold mine of information."

Tom Driver snorted derisively.

"You guys in counter-espionage are so hungry for something to do you'd be prepared to believe the devil was the Pope. More likely to be a gold mine of disinformation, if you ask me."

The older man flushed with obvious annoyance.

"Easy Tom. Remember where you are."

"Don't try pulling rank on me, Goodwin. Remember? This is the Security Service, not some bloody parade ground."

Brad, who had convened the meeting of the half dozen men in the Security Service whose advice he wanted and valued, laughingly intervened.

"Knock it off you two. You're both right and that's the measure of our problem, but it doesn't get us any nearer a solution to fight about it. John, what do you think?"

John Merrivale, the scholarly head of the Special Analysis group, took off his glasses and slowly rubbed his eyes.

"Well, Brad, as you say, both Tom and Sandy are right and that presents a problem. In a way, as I see it, we're damned if we do and we're damned if we don't. Whatever we recommend to the inter-departmental Committee on Defectors, we are bound to be crit-icized. If we recommend that Orion be admitted as a KGB defector on political grounds, we are going to be hard put to provide a satisfactory basis for the recommendation. There is a *prima facie* case for believing, as Tom appears to, that Orion is a plant. On the other hand, to recommend, out of hand, that we should reject him and turn him over to some other service before even the most rudimentary tests of his *bona fides* have been carried out would be rash — even unprofessional."

Brad smiled to himself as he listened. John Merrivale was no fool. By pointing out that any hasty rejection of Orion would be unprofessional, he was invoking the one argument which all of them would appreciate and accept. Not only would it be unprofessional, but it would be so considered by the various foreign intelligence and security agencies with which they had relations. That the argument would have little or no appeal outside the Security Service, es-pecially with Ministers, was another matter and a problem with which he would have to contend.

John Merrivale continued.

"On balance, I am inclined to think that we have more to lose than to gain by rejecting him before testing his story. True, it will require a considerable effort on our part and tie up valuable re-sources. But, as Tom has suggested, in the aftermath of the years of investigations and unfavourable publicity which the Security Ser-vice has received, those resources aren't being fully utilized any-way. However, for my money, in a sense Orion already has passed a test. Admittedly, it is a test of his creation and not ours and thus open to suspicion. Nevertheless, it has to be taken into considera-tion. He has asked to undergo facial surgery in order to protect himself from assassination by the KGB. Inquiries I have made from the medical profession indicate that the process is neither easy nor pleasant. In his case it will require hours of surgery, under full anaesthetic, spread over some time. Moreover, for someone as strikingly handsome as Molodny, the thought of transforming his features must be pretty repugnant. I find it hard to believe he would suggest such a thing without a very strong motive — in this case, apparently fear for his life. I say we should recommend his acceptance and be prepared to live with the consequences which flow from that decision."

Brad allowed the discussion to continue for another half-hour before thanking them for their advice and help. He asked George McCain to remain behind in the "cubby hole", the hidden retreat where they were meeting. Inherited by Brad from his predecessors, the facility, at first a closely guarded secret, became more widely known in the Security Service over the years. Nevertheless, access to it could only be had with Brad's authority and at his explicit invitation.

Visitors entered the "cubby hole" only through a sparsely furnished outer office, which was seldom used by Brad except for receiving "outsiders". A finger-print identification device installed inside the medicine cabinet in the bathroom of the outer office allowed access to the well-equipped, comfortable inner office. If the whorls and patterns of the right hand were recognized when it was pressed against a lighted, opaque glass panel in the medicine cabinet, a part of the bathroom wall slid noiselessly open to admit the visitor to a large, well-lit room. At the same time as the mechanism for opening the hidden door was activated, a small green light glowed on the desk of Brad's secretary who guarded the entrance to the outer office.

On the wall facing the entrance were five digital clocks showing the hour in five different time zones across the world. Overhead was a large screen and a variety of maps which could be quickly lowered by operating the array of coloured buttons on a small panel on the right hand side of the wall. To the extreme right and left were ranged Chubb filing cabinets fitted with dual combination locks. In the centre of the room was Brad's desk. At right angles to it was a small conference table with comfortable chairs around it. Brad and George McCain continued their conversation from there.

"You share Tom Driver's view — you think he's a phoney, don't you?"

"Well, I agree with Tom that there is something fishy about him. I don't trust the bastard, but I don't agree that we should turn him away without testing his story. As John Merrivale said, to do that would be unprofessional and probably not very smart in other terms."

Brad nodded his head in agreement.

"Whether or not we can get Ministers to agree to keep Orion, there are a number of things we have to do immediately. The first and the most important is to protect Paul and Patricia Gribanov. No matter what Ministers may decide to do about Orion, we have an obvious and immediate duty to protect those two. That means we will have to give them an entirely new identity again.. Whatever other message it contains, the Fabergé egg means that Galena

Nadya knows that Paul is alive and probably that he and Patricia are married. If she knows that, others also may know. Maybe even Orion knows. I would like you to put in train at once a complete change of identity for them. Move them to some other part of the country. I'll leave the choice of venue to you and the experts.

"The second thing is to reinforce the surveillance we have placed on Orion. I want full surveillance of him on a twenty-four hour basis. I also want everything he brought with him to be examined and re-examined down to the last safety pin. That should include a thorough physical examination — every orifice explored, every tooth X-rayed. The works."

George McCain grinned.

"We're ahead of you. We increased surveillance at the safe house last night and the medicos have already gone over him with a fine-tooth comb. They were to take him to the Tri-Service hospital this morning for a dental check-up, including X-rays of his teeth. They went over his clothing inch by inch, including that fancy belt he was wearing — the wide one with the mod looking brass buckle. They even took the stitching out and replaced it. As far as the surveillance teams are concerned, unless something shows up in the X-rays of his teeth, he's as clean as a whistle."

"Thanks, George. I should have known you'd be ahead of me."

"I'll have them start immediately on changing the identities of Paul and Patricia Gribanov."

George McCain hesitated.

"Something else on your mind, George?"

"Yes. Orion has made a request."

"A request? What kind of a request?"

"He wants a woman."

"He wants what?"

"A woman. You know, a female."

"The bastard. What the hell does he think we are, the KGB? Does he think we have a bunch of Canadian 'swallows' on our payroll?"

"I don't know, but it wouldn't be surprising if he did. What will I tell him?"

"Tell him to go to hell — that he's in Ottawa now, not Moscow. No, wait a minute. What was the name of that prostitute we used to our advantage a couple of years ago? She helped us with Operation Red Fox. Remember?"

"Remember? How the hell could I forget? Her name was Maisie, Maisie Donovan. She works the old market area. Quite a dish and bright. She was working her way through college. Kevin Doyle of the Ottawa Police morality squad put us on to her — she helps them from time to time. What have you in mind?"

"If Maisie was willing and the price was right, she might be able to give us a better handle on him. God knows how we would code the expenses in the accounts. "Entertainment" I expect, or "payment for services rendered". At least we wouldn't have the problem which that young duty officer in External faced when he was detailed to look after the entertainment of some visiting African head of state and ended up paying out of his own pocket for the call-girl he procured in the interest of maintaining good relations. The accounts people in External were scandalized when he asked to be reimbursed."

"Okay, I'll see what can be arranged. At least it should liven up the daily routine of the surveillance squad — especially the guys manning the TV monitors in the safe house. As good as those blue movies one gets in hotels these days, without having to pay for it. The girl — Maisie — will have to be told something about Orion. But what?"

"You're right. I leave that up to you and the surveillance team. I can't see any harm in telling her he's Russian. She'll probably figure that out for herself, although she might not. His English is pretty good. I assume you would take her to the safe house after dark. She probably wouldn't object to being blindfolded. Since, if the government agree to his staying in Canada, his appearance will be completely altered, it doesn't matter too much that she will know him as he is. He's the only one to lose from that."

"Agreed. From what the surveillance team have said, he is unlikely to be interested in small talk. He seems only to have one thing on his mind and Maisie is pretty experienced at that. If we are wrong, and he has some ulterior motive, we can be pretty certain that the audio surveillance at least, will pick up every sound. From her performance on Operation Red Fox, we can depend on Maisie to tell us about anything we don't pick up."

"Okay, George. Good luck. Keep me posted, although this is one aspect of the case that I do not anticipate mentioning to the Defectors Committee. I can see the expression on the face of the External Chairman if he were told about Maisie. He thinks of defectors in terms of the dictionary definition; blemished persons, better dealt with in the abstract."

As he was about to leave, George McCain stuck his head around the sliding door of the "cubby hole".

"By the way, I thought I might mention that we could probably pay for Maisie with a credit card."

Brad laughed.

"What the hell are you talking about?"

"I mean that the modern way to pay for such services is by

credit card. At least, that is what my friends on the morality squad tell me."

"You're kidding."

"No. If you don't believe me, look under the personal column in the newspapers. Usually under some heading like 'Introduction Services'. You know — 'Juanita, attractive blonde bombshell. Major credit cards', and then the telephone number. Even the oldest profession has had to modernize."

"Okay, use your credit card."

"Not mine. My wife and I have a joint one."

The sliding door shut as George McCain's grinning face disappeared.

The Chairman of the Defectors Committee wasn't exactly enthusiastic when Brad called him to ask for an emergency meeting.

"Can't it wait until our regularly scheduled meeting next month?"

" 'Fraid not Fred. We need a decision out of Ministers as soon as possible."

Fred Strachey, who had been stuck with the chairmanship by his department four years earlier and pined for a posting in some sophisticated European capital, sighed.

"Oh, all right. How about next Thursday?"

"How about this afternoon?"

"This afternoon? It's nearly noon now. Besides, I have a luncheon at the Austrian Chargé's. That won't be over before three at the earliest."

"Okay. How about three-thirty in your office?"

"I may be late."

"We'll wait. I'll 'phone the Immigration member, if you wish. I would also like to ask the ex-officio member from the Privy Council Office to be there. I think this eventually will end up on the Prime Minister's plate."

Brad was amused. As he had reckoned it might, mention of the Privy Council Office and the Prime Minister's possible interest caused a noticeable change in Fred Strachey's attitude and tone of voice.

"Well, if you think it is that important, perhaps we could meet earlier. I could excuse myself if we aren't through by two-thirty. How about three?"

"That would be better if you can manage it. We may have a lot to do in a hurry."

"Are there any papers?"

"No. It will be an oral briefing at this stage."

There was silence at the other end of the line as Fred Strachey digested the import of Brad's comment.

"Very well. At three in my office."

The Committee, formed years earlier during the cold war, had long outgrown its usefulness. It met infrequently and usually only to handle the kind of problems that could not be dealt with through some other part of the government apparatus. Nevertheless, it remained the only official forum where cases of the kind presented by Orion's defection could be safely handled at the inter-departmental level and before the interests of Ministers became engaged. As Brad anticipated, the reaction to Orion's defection and Brad's recommendation that he be granted political asylum was lukewarm. In the end, he received support from the representative from the Privy Council Office who, although he was an ex-officio member, had more clout than any of the others including Fred Strachey. As a result, the Committee agreed to have the matter placed before the Secretary to the Cabinet with the recommendation that it be raised with Ministers. The representative from the Privy Council Office was a former member of the Department of External Affairs with a background in intelligence work and a reputation for being tough-minded. Brad felt sure that it was due to his influence with the Secretary to the Cabinet that the matter was placed on the agenda of the next meeting of the Cabinet Committee on Security and Intelligence, scheduled for the following day.

Ministers on the Cabinet Committee were no more enthusiastic than officials at the idea of giving Orion sanctuary.

"How do we know he's genuine?"

Asked by the Prime Minister to reply to the question, Brad acknowledged that they did not know he was genuine and that this could not be known until he was thoroughly investigated. Brad also made it clear that even after intensive interrogation, doubts about his *bona fides* might remain. In the end, the decision to keep Orion in Canada was taken by the Prime Minister when, as the questioning of Brad continued, it became clear that if Canada was unwilling to have him, the Americans were prepared to give him immediate asylum. Indeed, Brad was able to say, on the basis of a telephone call he received from the Director of the CIA immediately before the meeting took place, that the agency was prepared to send a special aircraft to transport him to the United States that day. That did it.

The Prime Minister placed her long, manicured fingers together with her elbows on the table before her in a gesture very familiar to those who knew her, and looked around.

"Well, gentlemen. Are we agreed? I think we are quite capable of handling our own problems without help from our American friends. Mr. Randall, I assume you will want to get on with the task. Will the changing of the man's appearance take long?"

"The doctors say it should be a matter of weeks. They can't be more precise. If he is a quick healer, he will get through it quickly. If not, or if there are complications, it will take longer."

"I assume I will be kept informed?"

"I will make sure you are, Prime Minister."

Orion turned out to be a remarkably healthy specimen. His transformation was speedier than even the most optimistic medical opinion had estimated — and what a transformation it was! Brad visited the private clinic in Toronto twice. The first time Orion's face was swathed in bandages and he was being fed intravenously. He went back when the series of operations was completed and Orion was ready for release. On the second occasion Brad walked into the hospital room which was guarded by a member of the Security Service dressed in hospital garb. The room was empty.

"Where's he gone?"

"You just passed him in the corridor, Sir."

"Where?"

"There."

"My God. You mean that ugly bastard with the cauliflower ear?"

"The same."

Orion's toughness was attested to by the fact that barely a week after Brad's second visit to the clinic he was back in Ottawa securely installed in a couple of rooms on the fourth floor of RCMP headquarters in the guise of RCMP Corporal McCrea, on special assignment. The idea was the brainchild of John Merrivale.

"Why not? Can you think of a better disguise? The last place the KGB are likely to look for him is within the Force. On special assignment, he will have preferred status. The legend we create for him can make him a member of some Western detachment, assigned to headquarters. The fictitious paper work can be squared with the Divisional Commander concerned. His peers won't ask any questions and if he lives in Headquarters, he will be protected and kept under constant surveillance."

"With a good Scot's name like McCrea, the bastard might even turn out to be honest."

George McCain grinned like a Cheshire cat. Merrivale's Sassenach background prompted him to mutter,

"Merely a shift from one mafia to another."

"To hell with you, Merrivale."

What Molodny thought of the new role assigned him was

impossible to tell. He gave away almost nothing. Despite the contact lenses he was obliged to wear to change their colour, his eyes had a wary expression. He seemed mildly amused at the rank and role he had been given.

As soon as they could, the interrogation teams went to work on him. Brad had given a good deal of careful thought to the composition of the teams. Ideally, he felt there should be two teams, each consisting of two persons, taking turns in putting questions and complementing one another when the going got rough. One member of each team would adopt a sympathetic approach to Orion, while the other would take an aggressive stance.

Selecting the first pair of interrogators was easy. Stanley Hydchuck and Martin Loomis had worked together often and had some notable successes to their credit. They were the uncrowned heroes of Operation Short Fuse, which had resulted in breaking down the almost fool-proof cover story of a suspected "illegal". Stanley Hydchuck could be as tough as his six foot two frame and heavily muscled body suggested. At the same time, he could play the role of the sympathetic member of the team with conviction and feeling. After twenty-five years in the Security Service, there was little about his trade that he did not know. He had acquired an education the hard way, putting himself through university at his own expense during the days when anti-intellectualism was prevalent among many of the top brass in the Force. It had taken him seven years to complete his degree. He was among the top three in his graduating year — no mean feat for a man at least ten years older than anyone else in the class.

Martin Loomis was different. A Civilian Member, he had been recruited straight from university after completing an M.A. in psychology. He was fifteen years younger than Hydchuck. Despite the difference in their age and in their background they were good personal friends. Both possessed the instincts of the hunter, so necessary to the temperament of a good interrogator. They probably found some grim satisfaction in the fact that their latest quarry, Orion, was named after the hunter of Greek mythology.

Brad had greater difficulty in selecting the second interrogation team.

"George, I think Marcel Lepreau is an obvious choice. However, there isn't an experienced team-mate for him. Bruce Cowan would have been ideal since they worked together for so many years, but he's taken an early retirement and got a good job with one of the oil companies. A pity. We can't afford to lose that kind of experience. Any ideas?"

George McCain didn't answer immediately.

"Well, there is one possibility, but it won't appeal to everyone, least of all to Marcel Lepreau."

"What do you mean?"

"Use a woman."

"A woman? Can you think of any that would fill the bill?"

"Yes."

"Anyone particular in mind?"

"Yes, Patricia Haley."

"You mean the one we used as watchdog on Galena Nadya Gribanov during the 'Opal' case?"

"Yes."

"Has she any experience of interrogation work?"

"I would doubt it, but she has plenty of other experience. She is very intelligent and she's tough and resourceful. She has a black belt in judo and can certainly look after herself. Moreover, her familiarity with the Opal case would be an advantage in dealing with Orion."

"Interesting."

"I have a hunch that it might throw Orion off stride to have a woman interrogator. However, it may be a non-starter."

"Why?"

"Well, Marcel Lepreau isn't exactly noted for being an admirer of women. You've heard him often enough on the subject of women's lib and the place of women in society. His views on the subject make the Ayatollah Khomeini sound like Nellie McClung."

"Yes, I've heard him on the subject but I think that's more a reflection of his own rather messy marriage and divorce than of his true convictions. I wonder if he's as anti-feminist as he pretends."

"Maybe."

"Anyway, it's a brilliant idea. Let's try it, if it doesn't work, all we've lost is some time."

In the end, to Brad's surprise, both Lepreau and Haley welcomed the suggestion, apparently regarding the proposal as a personal challenge. By the time they were ready to take up the slack for Hydchuck and Loomis, the interrogation of Orion had fallen into a regular daily pattern. At the outset he had proven to be a difficult subject. He volunteered nothing, making his interrogators work for everything they extracted from him. As Hydchuck told Brad after they had been at it a week,

"He's tough. Tough and clever. He hasn't given away one damn thing that he hasn't wanted to let us have. He is constantly probing and testing us. I only got the bastard off balance once. Occasionally he has pleaded ignorance of English and lapsed into Russian. On such occasions we have patiently brought him back to the question and extracted an answer in English. However, yesterday he tried the same tack in an obvious attempt to irritate us. I let him have it with both barrels in fluent Russian. I told him to stop playing games; that the interrogation was to take place in English and that I was well aware that his English was at least as good as my Russian. That stopped him in his tracks. It's the first time I have seen him flustered. Since, for the purpose of the interviews, I have been using the name Stanley Welch, he obviously had no idea I could speak his language. He's an arrogant son of a bitch but he isn't invulnerable."

"Is he genuine?"

"Too early to tell. Certainly nothing he has told us so far would allow us to make a judgment one way or the other. He's spinning it out — but that's normal behaviour for most defectors. As you know, we have got beyond the name, rank and serial number phase. His story of the early days of his recruitment and training has the ring of truth about it. But even if it was all fabricated, we have no means of testing it. The basic data is being made available to the Brits and the Americans, who have some material on him, but I would be very surprised if there are significant discrepancies. He's far too professional to make basic mistakes of that kind, assuming he isn't what he pretends to be; someone who has defected for ideological reasons."

When the team of Marcel Lepreau and Patricia Haley took up where the first team left off, a situation developed which none of them had quite foreseen. Brad felt immediately that they could exploit it to their advantage. Patricia Haley surprised everyone by the ease with which she took to the work. It became clear that even Orion was unaware that she had no previous experience of interrogation techniques. More important, although she made every effort to conceal it from Orion, his appearance repelled her. Through the strange chemistry which forges a bond between interrogator and interrogee, Orion sensed Patricia's repulsion. His vanity was piqued. For a man who had been as handsome as Molodny, to find himself physically repulsive to a woman as beautiful and intelligent as Patricia Haley must have been a traumatic experience. Unable to prevent himself, he made an effort to attract her — to please her. Thus, almost against his will, he became a more malleable subject and the course of the interrogation speeded up. They came more quickly to the reasons why the Security Service had been so eager to interrogate him in the first place — his initial statement that there were three KGB spies working in the Canadian government apparatus, whom he could not identify precisely. It was the hope that Orion's interrogation might provide sufficient leads to uncover all three spies.

Patricia shifted her body in the chair and re-crossed her legs. The Russian's eyes followed the move.

"Well, Igor, you were mentioning before lunch that you thought that some of the reports you had seen from one of the agents, dealt with Cabinet business. Why did you think that?"

"Reports said so."

"What do you mean?"

"Gave views of different members of government — of Canadian politburo."

"Cabinet Ministers?"

"Yes, yes. Cabinet Ministers. Their talk about wheat trade with Soviet Union."

"When was this?"

"Don't know. Must be three years ago. Maybe more. Also talk on Canadian politburo position on negotiations at Geneva."

"You mean disarmament?"

"No, no. Trading. Tariffs."

"You mean the GATT negotiations?"

"Yes, GATT. At Geneva."

"Was the spy a man or a woman?"

"Man."

"How do you know?"

"I learned."

"How?"

"Someone tell me."

"Who?"

"Don't remember. Someone in First Chief Directorate."

"You can't remember the person's name?"

"No, can't remember."

"Young or old?"

"Don't know."

Inexorably, slowly, bit by bit the teams extracted information which built up a profile. Someone with access to Cabinet documents, a number of which dealt with international trade matters, including wheat sales to Russia. If Orion was to be believed, the spy was a male; age, appearance, background and precise occupation all unknown. Further interrogation by Hydchuck and Loomis suggested the agent also had access to a specific Cabinet document dealing with government policies on the sale of nuclear reactors. In particular, the interrogators were able to pin-point an approximate date since Orion claimed the document discussed sales of nuclear fuels to India. This led to a particular piece of paper. From the distribution list they were able to identify all those to whom the document was circulated officially — a list of fifty-two names. Unfortunately, as was so often the case with such documents, it turned out there were at least an additional twenty names of persons with unofficial access.

At an earlier stage, it became clear that Orion possessed information of interest to the British and Americans. They each sent experts who interrogated him with a member of the RCMP

Security Service present. Orion provided them with apparently promising leads to Russian spies who might have penetrated the British and American intelligence communities. In the case of the Americans, Orion even provided a physical description. The information he provided the British was more tenuous but suggested a penetration of the British defence establishment.

Reading the transcripts of those interrogations, Brad had the uneasy feeling that Orion had been more forthcoming with the British and the Americans than he had with his Canadian captors. He noticed with irritation that the synopsis of the interrogation by the British spoke of a "mole" in the British defence establishment. He knew that the term, first given currency by authors of spy fiction, had gained acceptance in the real world of spies, but he wished it hadn't. Next thing would probably be an attempt by some author to give the term a gender; a male "spy in place" would be described as a mole, a female "spy in place" would be known as a vole. Brad snorted derisively and turned back to his uneasiness at Orion's forthrightness. He spoke to George McCain.

"Yes. The same thought crossed my mind. We've been at the bastard for weeks and we haven't got nearly as much out of him as he appears to have given the Brits and the Americans in two days. However, the fault may lie in the eye of the beholder. Perhaps, because of our peculiar situation, we are becoming slightly paranoid. I can't see any particular reason why he would deliberately hold back on us while practically volunteering information to our friends. What purpose would that serve? I can't think of any."

Brad sighed.

"I guess you're right, George. Perhaps the case is getting to me."

* * * * * * * * * * * * * * * * * * *

The Cessna taxied noisily to a halt in front of the Department of Transport hangar at Uplands airport — described in rather grand and exaggerated terms as "Ottawa International Airport". Brad unbuckled his seat-belt and stretched. He felt satisfied that he had spent the time of the flight to advantage. He would try to see the Prime Minister as soon as possible. It was one time his right of direct access might be made to pay off.

Three

As Brad drove the unmarked Security Service Ford LTD along the narrow dirt road running around the western shore of Meach Lake, enroute to the Prime Minister's country house at the more distant Harrington Lake, a refrain ran through his mind:

Sugar and Spice,
and all things nice.
That's what little girls are made of.

The Prime Minister may once have been a little girl but she certainly was never made of "sugar and spice and all things nice". Salt and pepper might be a better description. He wondered how she would react to Matt Villiers information and if she would accept the trust he placed in Villiers. On the basis of past performance Brad hoped and expected that she might understand. He marvelled that with all her other responsibilities she was able also to deal so fully and effectively with questions of national security.

He drew up before the locked gate barring the road to casual sightseers. He noted the TV camera to the left of the gate — a silent sentinel set on a metal post overlooking the entrance. An RCMP constable awaited him having been alerted by Brad's call made over the radio-telephone in his car.

"Good morning, constable."

"Morning, Sir. Going to be a great day. A flock of Canada geese just went over."

"Missed them. Guess that means winter isn't far off."

Brad drove the remainder of the short distance to the large, rambling house which had been used by successive Prime Ministers of Canada since 1959. The incongrous ditty still ran through his head as he parked his car. He hoped that he wasn't making a mistake in approaching the Prime Minister directly over the Orion affair. If she concluded that he had abused his unwritten right to direct access to her, she would tell him so in no uncertain terms.

"Good morning, Mr. Randall."

"Good morning, Prime Minister."

"You wanted to see me? I assume it has to do with your favourite Russian defector?"

"Yes, Prime Minister. It is about Orion. As the Secretary to the Cabinet will have told you, he provided the Americans and the British with leads which suggested the Russians have managed to infiltrate their respective intelligence communities. He also will have told you that our investigations have not progressed as quickly as we hoped but that the information he has provided points in certain directions."

"Well?"

"Because we learned that the leads the Americans received looked very promising, I made a quick trip to Washington to talk to the CIA. Often one can learn more from an hour's talk face to face than from pages of telegraphic reports. Officially, my trip was a waste of time. Unofficially, I learned through a friend of long standing, who stuck his neck out in telling me, that Orion's information led directly to a Russian spy in a branch of the National Security Agency — their top secret wireless interception and cypher breaking outfit. They were able to get a confession from him within hours of his arrest. More important, he led them to a possible spy within the Central Intelligence Agency — in the most senior levels of that organization. Understandably, the Americans are in a state of disarray and quite unwilling at this stage of their investigations to disclose their problems even to their friends and allies."

The Prime Minister said nothing.

"Not surprisingly, my friend — the one who provided me with this information — was only willing to do so on the explicit understanding that I would not divulge it to anyone else in Canada. Eventually, when I pointed out to him that the information would have no value unless I could communicate it to those having to take decisions, he agreed I might tell you — it being understood that the secret would remain with you and me until we had the information from some other source."

"What decision do you expect of me?"

"Well, Prime Minister, what my friend told me seems to establish Orion's credibility in a way which we have so far been unable to do. He has provided valuable information of current worth — not something which is hopelessly outdated. This suggests strongly that he is genuine — that he is what he claims to be — a senior KGB officer willing to provide us with information of value in return for sanctuary and protection. He claims his motives are largely ideological. We can't test that claim yet. But, if he can provide us with information of the kind he has given the Americans, his motivation for doing so is of secondary importance."

Brad paused. The Prime Minister remained silent. Brad continued.

"Our interrogation of Orion to date indicates that one of the three spies he claims he has heard of in the Canadian government is someone with access to certain Cabinet documents — even the minutes of Cabinet discussions."

"You mean someone in my office or in the Privy Council Office?"

"We don't know, Prime Minister. More likely it is someone in a ministry dealing with international trade. We have recently identified one Cabinet document dealing with government policy on the sale of nuclear reactors, which Orion certainly knew the content of. Unfortunately, there are at least seventy persons who had access to it. Of these, about twenty-five are Ministers or of deputy-minister rank."

"Do you suspect any of them?"

"At this stage I suspect everyone who had access to the document. It is not a very pretty situation and it may take some time for us to narrow down the list of suspects."

"How will you do that?"

"There are many possibilities. For example, if we can identify another document we might be able to narrow our list to those who had access to both pieces of paper."

"I see."

The Prime Minister rose and walked across the living room to the window overlooking the lake. She remained there for some time before walking back to where Brad was seated.

"I suppose you have been wondering if you did the right thing in coming to me directly?"

"Yes. Frankly, Prime Minister, it was a difficult decision to take. I have always tried not to abuse the privileges of direct access to you. It seemed to me, however, that this was one occasion when I should exercise the privilege."

"Put your mind at rest, Mr. Randall. I am glad you decided to take the risk involved."

Her lips parted in a wry smile as she pronounced the word "risk".

The thought flashed through Brad's mind, as he heard her words with relief, that she might be a tough lady but she was not without the ability to poke fun at herself.

"Exactly what do you want me to decide?"

"Whether the Security Service can investigate those we suspect. Eventually, to be successful, we may have to have authority to use the most intrusive methods. This could involve intercepting the communications of Ministers and senior officials. Have we your agreement to do this?"

"Yes, you have my agreement. I assume you are satisfied the information you received is accurate?"

"I have no doubts on that score. I have known the man for years and I trust him."

"Good, I will inform the Secretary to the Cabinet that I have authorized you to investigate a number of persons, including, possibly, Ministers and senior officials. I will simply tell him that I am doing so on the basis of information you have made available to me. I will inform him you are to seek my personal authority before any intrusive methods of investigation are used against members of the Cabinet or deputy-ministers. Is that agreeable?"

"Perfectly, Prime Minister."

"Will your investigations include your own Minister?"

"His was not one of the names of persons to whom the Cabinet document I mentioned was circulated. I am relieved on that score."

"Fortuitous, I agree, although I understand there have been occasions in the past when the Minister responsible for the Security Service has been the object of an investigation by the RCMP?"

"I believe so, Prime Minister. Not during my time."

"Exactly, Mr. Randall. We live in an imperfect world. Thank you for coming to see me. I expect to be kept informed."

Before Brad could reply, she had turned and made her way through the living room door leading to the back of the house.

Immediately following his talk with the Prime Minister, Brad spoke personally with all those in the Security Service who were involved in the Orion case. Without disclosing anything of his discussions with Matt Villiers, he indicated the Prime Minister agreed they might investigate any of those persons who, as a result of Orion's information, appeared to be likely candidates. He gave explicit instructions that knowledge of the investigations was to be confined to the Security Service and within it on a strictly "need to know" basis. He issued further instructions that no intrusive surveillance methods were to be employed without his personal approval and made clear that any such methods employed against Ministers or those of the rank of deputy-minister or the equivalent would have to be approved by the Prime Minister. He made it abundantly clear that his own Minister was not privy to the investigations and that he was not to be made privy to them. In talking to his immediate advisers, he stressed the need to exhaust every avenue of investigation open to them before resorting to more clandestine methods.

"Our first task is to whittle down the present large and unwieldy list of suspects. That can only be done through a painstaking process of educated elimination. We probably will need help from those in the bureaucracy who are versed in matters of international trade, wheat sales and our policies on the sale of nuclear reactors and nuclear fuels — particularly the latter. Obviously, we will have to have a credible cover story to disguise the real reasons for our inquiries. Perhaps hints which suggest a criminal investigation involving some vague, unspecified infringement of the law will suffice. Careful thought will have to be given to this aspect. A hint of criminal investigation has the advantage that no politician getting wind of it will want to have anything to do with it for fear of being accused of interfering with the course of justice. I leave it to you fellows to come up with something credible. Keep me in the picture."

Brad made a special point of speaking to each of the four interrogators, since their ability to squeeze details out of Orion might prove to be crucial. His conversation with Patricia Haley was particularly helpful.

"The fact that you don't like the man — that you find him repulsive — is a plus. Don't worry about it, Patricia. As you have pointed out, he senses your physical revulsion — he's no fool. Keep on just as you have. It has begun to pay off. He is trying to please you and in the process, he has become a hell of a lot more cooperative."

"I hope you are right. I can't help it. He just gives me the creeps."

"Is it his appearance? The doctors were very successful."

"I don't know. Certainly, he is no beauty in his new guise. There is something about the man that I don't like. I think it goes deeper than mere appearance. Something happened the other day, when Marcel and I were questioning him, that may explain it."

"What was that?"

"Marcel left the room for some reason while I was interrogating him. Orion was sitting in the chair by the window. I noticed a large black spider — one of those ones with repulsive, long black hair on it. The thing was the size of a quarter. To my horror, it landed on his neck from the curtain-rod above. I can't stand spiders in any form. I let out a yell pointing to the filthy thing. He paid no attention. Just went on answering my question. He let the creature walk around his neck and onto his collar without paying any attention to it. He's inhuman. Finally, the thing jumped off his arm onto the floor. I stamped on it. He just smiled. I felt an utter fool."

"Interesting. Most interesting. I share your dislike of spiders. I would have reacted in much the same way as you did."

The two teams continued their interrogation of Orion.

"You say that co-ordination of joint operations by the Czechs, the Poles and Moscow Centre was carried out through Prague?"

"Yes. Only some operations."

"Why Prague?"

"StB, Czech secret police, used for disinformation operations in Europe. Not America. Operations against America controlled from Moscow Centre."

"Do you know of any such operations?"

"No."

"Yet you know they took place from Prague and Moscow?"

"Yes. Also some operations against America done with Cuban Intelligence Service. Probably also against Canada."

"Do you have information about such operations? About specific operations?"

"No. No specific operations."

Orion paused to take a sip of coffee.

"Recruitment operations against foreigners in eastern Europe done through Sofia."

"Sofia?"

"Yes, with Bulgarian intelligence people. KGB carried out some Department V operations through Sofia."

"You mean using Bulgarian operatives."

"Yes, Bulgarian operatives. Also training. Big training school near Sofia."

"What kind of training school?"

"Espionage and sabotage."

Day after day it continued. The transcripts grew voluminous. They concentrated most of their efforts on trying to get Orion to be more precise about the three spies he claimed were operating in Canada. They hammered away trying to extract information from him about any Cabinet documents. Did he remember any direct quotes in reports he had seen? Did he know anything about the frequency of such reports? How were they received? Did they seem to be the work of one person or more? Invariably, his answer was;

"Don't know. Can't remember."

He did add snippets of information. For example, he remembered that one of the documents was code-named, although he couldn't remember the name. He said he thought it had been routed to Moscow Centre through Havana, but he wasn't certain. It was frustrating and the interrogators were showing the strain despite the fact that they were able to take turns in the questioning. Orion on the other hand seemed indestructible. He thrived on the routine established for him. Patricia Haley decided to take him over the ground again — ground they already had covered several times.

Marcel Lepreau left the room to make some more coffee in the small kitchen across the hall.

"Igor, you have said you thought one of the documents you saw was routed through Havana."

"Yes, Havana."

"How would you know that?"

"Routing instructions. Call sign for Havana."

"Do you remember that?"

"Think so. Not sure."

"It was a cable?"

"No. Wireless."

"How do you know?"

"Call sign only used for wireless."

"You remember then seeing a wireless message which you think was from Havana?"

"Yes."

He looked eagerly at Patricia. She tried not to let her feelings show in her face. He was at his most repulsive when he was trying to ingratiate himself with her. He looked at her with a sly smile.

"Remember name."

She tried to suppress her excitement.

"Igor, what name?"

"Code-name."

"You mean code-name on the document from Havana?"

"Yes."

"What was it?"

"Zherebéts."

"What does that mean in English?"

"Don't know."

"Can't you give me some idea?"

He leered at her in a particularly repulsive way, pointing to a calendar on the wall depicting the RCMP musical ride.

"Horse."

"It means horse?"

He made a rude gesture with his forearm thrust into his crotch.

"Horse. Male horse."

Patricia felt her cheeks flush. Damn the repulsive bastard.

"You mean a stallion?"

At that moment, to her relief, Marcel Lepreau re-joined them with three cups of hot coffee. She quickly filled him in on what Orion had told her.

"I'll check with Stanley. We'll get him to write the Russian word on a piece of paper, then we'll take a break. You look as if you could use one."

Brad read the interrogation team's report with more than usual interest when George McCain brought it to the next Orion staff meeting.

"Stallion. What the hell does that mean?"

"I looked up the English dictionary, which defines a stallion as an "uncastrated horse, especially one kept for breeding". In Alberta, where I was brought up, it was used to denote unusual sexual prowess — not in a pejorative sense either. It also was used to describe someone of unusual strength or a man who was 'well hung', as they used to say."

"Where does that lead us? Do you mean to say we have to seek out those on our list of suspects who are well hung? How the hell do I explain that to the Prime Minister. Surely the bastard is leading us up the garden path? Having a good laugh at our expense. He's playing with us."

"I'm not so sure, Brad. It's not impossible. Even the KGB may have a sense of humour in their use of code-names. We've certainly had some fun on that score. Remember the guy from the Polish Embassy, the senior UB officer, who we turned after he was discovered as a 'found in' during a police raid on a male bordello in Toronto? We ran him successfully for over a year. He was given the code-name Wild Card. Some more literary-minded member dealing with the case added an 'e' on the Wild to honour the memory of Oscar Wilde. It's quite possible we are looking for a 'stallion' on the list."

"Okay, have a go at it. But I'll be damned if I'm going to raise it with the Prime Minister."

Immediately the list became shorter. Eliminating all women cut it by eighteen. Many other names were eliminated simply because they couldn't possibly fit the criteria suggested by Orion's testimony. Eventually, the list was narrowed down to five suspects. One of these was a Cabinet Minister, whose reputation as a stud was legendary. Two were senior public servants in ministries with an interest in atomic energy matters, the fourth was a senior executive in a Crown corporation and the fifth was a political appointee, a member of the exempt staff of a Minister involved in international trade matters. All of them had or could have gained access to the Cabinet document in question. Indeed, in the case of the Cabinet Minister and the two public servants their signatures were on file as acknowledging receipt of the document. All five were well known for their sexual exploits.

The Cabinet Minister, the two public servants and the Crown corporation executive had all received security clearances. Hence, there was a good deal of information available on RCMP files about them. Since they were all cleared to Top Secret, extensive field investigations of their various backgrounds were on file. With the exception of the Crown corporation executive, none of the enquiries extended beyond Canada. In his case, since he had served for a period as a member of the NATO secretariat, his file contained reports from overseas agencies, including the NATO Security Bureau. Although there was nothing in the reports to suggest any involvement with hostile intelligence services, he had enjoyed a particularly torrid love affair with an Italian working in the NATO registry in the few months before his wife and children joined him in Brussels. From the photographs accompanying the report, it was easy to see what had attracted him to her. As George McCain remarked,

"Boy, she's stacked. Reminds me of the flight deck of a U.S. aircraft carrier."

Since exempt staff of Ministers were political appointments, they were not required to have security clearances. The theory was that such employees did not have access to classified documents — their principal function being to assist Ministers with the political aspects of their portfolio. In practice, however, since much of the work which flowed through a Minister's office inevitably had domestic political overtones — the sale of nuclear reactors, for example — the theory had little application in reality. It was a weakness in the system which the Security Service had pointed out over the years, but which Ministers were unwilling to correct since to do so might limit their ability to pay off political debts. There was, therefore, nothing on the RCMP's files about Peter Gustav Gadenus, the fifth man on their short list.

"Since we have a relative wealth of information about the first four on our list and virtually nothing about Gadenus, I suggest our first task should be to correct that discrepancy. It seems that all we know about him is that he came to Canada from Hungary in 1956 with his parents. He was seventeen at the time. His father has since died and his mother is living in Kitchener. We know this from being able to have an unofficial look at his House of Commons application for an identity card and their payroll documentation. We know little more except that he has a reputation with the ladies — it appears that he and one of the secretaries from the office of some MP were caught *in flagrante delecto* as it were, by one of the cleaning women, who reported it to the House of Commons security staff. They took no action, but we learned about it from one of them. We have his present address, his social insurance number, the license number of his car, and his telephone number. That's about it."

Brad paused to look at those assembled in the "cubby hole" to discuss the matter. George McCain spoke.

"If we are going to find out the things that count without arousing the curiosity of others and his suspicions, we will have to resort to intrusive methods. The only other alternative is to pull him in for questioning. But on what grounds? If he is a spy he'll be

warned and there is no way we can prevent him from skipping the
country. If he is not a spy he will holler to high heaven and we will
have his Minister on our backs at once. The Prime Minister is
unlikely to appreciate that."

"Your're right, George. We really don't have much choice.
Okay. Given the fact that he is a political appointment, I must
inform the Prime Minister of our suspicions and get her permission
to use intrusive methods against him. In any event, I will require
warrants and in the present situation, the only Minister who can
sign is the Prime Minister. As soon as the paper work can be
prepared, I will try to see her."

The Prime Minister received Brad in her Centre Block office
overlooking the grassy, open spaces before the buildings of parliament where, in the summer months, the changing of the guard
ceremony is staged every week-day, to the delight of tourists. As
Brad looked out the window before taking the seat indicated to him
by the Prime Minister, the grass was hidden by a good eighteen
inches of snow.

"Well, Mr. Randall. Have you something to report?"

Brad quickly sketched in the results of their investigations of
Gadenus and the reasons why they wished to carry them one step
further. She reacted to Brad's description of the KGB code-name
with amusement.

"I know Gadenus. He was helpful in my riding in the last
election. Politically astute. A good organizer. The sobriquet 'stallion' might be appropriate in his case, but from what I have heard,
'billy-goat' might be better. He is not a very tall man, but he
obviously has great physical stength — huge legs and shoulders.
Like a wrestler. Do you think he could be a spy?"

"I simply don't know, Prime Minister. Certainly, we have
nothing at present to suggest he is. Through surveillance — interception of his communications — we hope to be able to make some
judgment."

"You want me to authorize you to carry out such surveillance?"

"Yes, Prime Minister. I have prepared the necessary warrants
for your signature."

The Prime Minister accepted the documents without comment. Signing them, she returned them to Brad.

"Keep me informed."

She turned to the pile of papers on the desk before her.
Familiar with this form of dismissal, Brad withdrew, quietly closing
the heavy oak door behind him.

Four

The Russian tank commander turned his flashlight to shine onto the face of his steel-cased wrist watch. As the minute hand swept forward to mark 4 a.m. he spoke slowly into the throat microphone. The guttural words could be heard by members of his tank crew below him.

"Advance. Objective — Green line. Out."

As he finished speaking, the diesel engine kicked over sullenly in the cold morning air — once, twice. The third time, the engine burst into life with a deep-throated roar. Greasy diesel fumes filled the small space into which the four man crew was squeezed. The metal bulk of the T-54 lurched forward, churning up the soft earth of the bivouac, as it turned onto the hard surface of the road leading north to Budapest. The remaining tanks of the regiment fell into line after the lead tank, their headlights stabbing the darkness between them, careless of the need for black-out precautions. Their prospective enemy; a motley collection of factory workers, students and elements of the Hungarian army who possessed no aircraft, no anti-tank artillery, no helicopters — nothing which posed an organized threat to the steel monsters. The date was November 4, 1956.

Earlier that year the ferment which, in late October, was to produce such an intoxicating and dangerous political brew had begun to work. Discontent already was in the air by the time the intense heat of summer descended upon the city like a wet blanket causing a pervasive stench in the old part of Pest from sewers set too close to the surface. Writers, journalists and a sprinkling of intellectuals, the majority Communists and Communist sympathizers, increasingly expressed their dislike of Mátyas Rákosi's regime. Ironically the intellectual inspiration for the revolution came from Communist rather than anti-Communist elements. In the Spring of 1956, when the Petöfi Circle debates were thrown open to the public, a forum was created for the expression of opposition to the unpopular regime of Rákosi. Khrushchev's secret speech to the Twentieth Party Congress in Moscow, denouncing Stalin, led shortly after to Rákosi's ouster and his replacement by a reluctant Imre Nagy who naively believed in a humanistic Communism in which the Party becomes a sacred vessel containing noble-minded disciples of Marx ready to let the state wither away.

October 6, 1956 was unpleasantly cold and windy in Budapest, yet over 200,000 people turned out at the Kerepesi cemetery to commemorate 13 Hungarian generals hanged on that day in 1849 by the Hapsburgs in a successful effort to crush the Magyar War of Independence. Significantly, on that occasion the Hapsburgs had been helped by the Russians. The commemoration ceremony turned out to be a dress rehearsal for the full scale revolution which began seventeen days later on October 23.

Early in the morning of October 23, the Communist Party newspaper, *Szabad Nép,* supporting an initiative by students calling for a number of freedoms then denied by the regime, was being sold on the streets. Twelve hours later the monstrous 26 foot statue of Stalin in the city's centre was toppled. Parts of it were dragged through the streets eventually to lie in the Adrassy ut, Budapest's main thoroughfare. The radio building was beseiged by crowds of angry insurgents. Steel-helmeted members of the AVH (Állam-védelmi Hatóság) the State Security police, carrying rifles, defended the building and were stationed at strategic points throughout the city. Three Hungarian army light tanks moved slowly into Sardor utca, a street so narrow it would have been difficult for two large American cars side by side to squeeze into it. The hatches of the tanks were open and the tank crews were unhelmeted, smiling and fraternizing with the crowds surrounding them. By midnight the sound of sporadic automatic rifle fire could be heard on the east bank of the Danube in Pest — the air reeked of tear gas. The scene around the radio building became ugly when the crowd discovered that an ambulance, which had edged its way through the crowd towards the building, contained automatic weapons intended for the AVH members defending it.

By 2 a.m. Soviet T-34 tanks, with markings indicating they came from Soviet camps 100 kilometres from Budapest, appeared in the centre of the city, taking up positions at bridges and other strategic points. On October 25 massive demonstrations were held in Liberty Square and in front of the Parliament buildings. About two dozen Russian tanks took up positions around the square and the roads leading to it. The atmosphere was friendly, the tank crews chatting with the crowds. Then a sudden burst of automatic rifle fire hit a number of the tanks, wounding several of the Russians. The tank crews reacted in panic — abandoning their wounded they closed the hatches, and rotating their gun turrets rapidly, fired wildly in all directions. Many in the crowd were killed and wounded; bodies littered the square, the pavement was spattered with blood.

For the next ten days Hungary was in turmoil. Known members of the hated AVH were hunted down and killed, some by hanging from lamposts in the centre of Budapest. The words *"Ruszki haza"* (Russians go home) were chalked on walls throughout the city. Freedom Fighters, as they then became known, many of them in their early teens, attacked the Russians with small arms fire and with homemade Molotov cocktails. The latter weapons were used most effectively by young boys and girls. Shod in worn running shoes, resembling latter day Minoan Bull dancers, they leapt onto Russian tanks with swift daring, knocking them out of action with well-placed gasoline bombs.

By the time the heavy Russian tanks, the T-54's, part of two divisions ordered up from Romania, appeared in the city with their guns sticking out before them like monstrous steel erections ejaculating 155 mm shells, the days of the Freedom Fighters were numbered. Points of resistance, barricades, buildings and army barracks were literally obliterated by tank gun-fire and artillery shells. Later, Russian soldiers armed with automatic rifles hunted down their opponents and killed them, hanging some from lamposts in retaliation for the hangings of members of the AVH in the two preceding weeks.

Gadenus, his wife and their only son Péter Gustav, were able to stay out of trouble in the weeks before the revolution and when full scale fighting broke out between Russians and Hungarian patriots. Their small house in a residential district on the slopes of Rozsadomb (Hill of Roses) remained untouched and father and son, both of whom were secretly in the pay of the AVH, managed to pose successfully as strong supporters of the revolution. The small shop where Ernö Gadenus carried on his trade as a watchmaker and jeweller was destroyed by gun-fire and the subsequent flames which engulfed it and several buildings on either side. Gadenus was able to salvage little from the rubble. He draped the front door of their row house with a red, white and green Hungarian flag from the centre of which the Soviet type coat of arms had been crudely cut out.

Ernö Gadenus was a long time secret member of the executive of the Hungarian Communist Party who, over the years, also performed various tasks for the AVH. His association with the State Security Service began soon after it was first created by the Russians in 1945 and when it was headed by Gábor Péter, whose real name was Benö Auspitz. Auspitz mysteriously disappeared on a Sunday afternoon in January, 1953. There were those who believed that his disappearance was engineered by Vladimir Parker, a Russian secret police officer detailed to Hungary.

Ernö's son, Péter Gustav, first came to the attention of the AVH when he was in his early teens. He was accused of rape by the mother of an attractive fifteen-year-old girl working in a state bicycle factory. The AVH, partly because he was Ernö's son, used their hidden influence to have the charges quashed. The price for their help, however, was Péter Gustav's recruitment as an informer. Subsequently, he was employed on specific tasks, some of them unsavoury. In return for his continued co-operation, the AVH pandered to his extraordinary sexual appetites. Eventually, when he became known to the NKVD, his sexual prowess earned him the Russian nickname "Stallion".

Ernö and Péter Gadenus were not surprised, therefore, to be summoned to an AVH house in Buda on the morning of November 3, 1956. The building was one of a number taken over by the AVH following the sacking of their former vast headquarters in the city centre. Father and son were ushered into a room on the top floor of the building.

"Come in. Please sit down."

The man speaking was a Hungarian, a member of the AVH known to Péter Gustav as Strabo. Neatly dressed in a dark grey suit, a white shirt and a pearl grey tie, he was overshadowed by his two companions who had an unmistakable Russian air about them. Both were dressed in badly fitting blue suits with very wide cuffs to their trousers. The shorter of the two had light blue eyes and closely-cropped, sand-coloured hair. The second man was about fifteen centimetres taller than his companion. He had a sallow complexion, gold filled teeth and shrewd, beady black eyes.

"These gentlemen" — he managed to give the word a slightly sarcastic inflection in Hungarian — "want to talk to you. They are from Moscow. I will leave you."

The door closed behind Strabo. The shorter of the two Russians spoke Hungarian with a heavy Russian accent.

"Tomorrow there will be fighting — heavy fighting. The rebels will be killed. Many of your countrymen will seek to flee. Many already have crossed into Austria. Most of them we wish to see leave. Some we will stop. You — you both — will join those leaving Hungary. We want you to become refugees. Make your way to Vienna. You will be interned and placed in a refugee camp."

He paused as Ernö Gadenus tried to interrupt him.

"Yes?"

"What about my wife? I can't leave her behind."

"She goes too."

"What will we do in Austria?"

"You only stay there until you can be accepted elsewhere as a refugee — you must try to be accepted into the United States or Canada."

"What will we do for money?"

"The U.N. refugee organization will look after you."

This last comment was made almost contemptuously.

"When you need additional money, we will provide it. You will be contacted."

"When do we have to leave?"

"Tomorrow."

"Tomorrow? That won't give us time to pack anything."

"Refugees aren't expected to have a lot of luggage. You will be a refugee. The less you carry the better."

"What about my shop?"

"I understand it has been destroyed — burned to the ground and anything of value looted. You will be recompensed in due course. The Party will look after that."

"What about papers — passports?"

"They will be provided. Better you keep your own names. My colleague will have papers for the three of you tomorrow morning."

He waved his hand in the direction of the taller of the two who was watching them with unblinking eyes.

"But why tomorrow? What's the rush?"

Impatience and anger showed in the blue eyes of the man who had done all the talking.

"Because tomorrow the Russian army will take over — will attack. It has been decided. Politburo members Anastas Mikoyan, Georgi Zhukov and Mikhail Suslov are here now with Soviet Ambassador Yuri Andrópov."

The two Gadenuses said nothing, digesting what they had heard.

"You stay here, now. Not safe to be in city."

"But what about my wife?", exclaimed Ernö.

"She will be brought here. Tomorrow the three of you will be driven out of the city towards Sopron, where many have been "escaping". You will join those seeking to get into Austria. When you are established as refugees, you will be contacted."

The taller of the two took out a crumpled packet of American cigarettes, extracted a cigarette with long, nicotine-stained fingers, placed it between his lips and lit it with an obviously expensive silver lighter. He did not offer cigarettes to the others. Péter Gustav spoke.

"What are we to do if we get to the United States or Canada?"

"You will be contacted when the time comes — if you are successful in being selected. You will have to pass yourself off as being younger than you are — it may not be that easy. You haven't exactly got the appearance of a schoolboy and, from what I hear, no medical examiner will use the word 'pubescent' to describe you."

Péter Gustav smiled crookedly, appearing to take the comment as a compliment. The Russian reacted sharply.

"We will be spending a good deal of effort and money on you

Péter. We don't want you screwing around. Keep it in your pants until you get to America."

Gadenus senior flushed and started to say something but decided against it when he caught the look in the Russian's eyes. Péter looked sullen and defiant but remained silent.

The Gadenus family, in the company of thousands of other fleeing Hungarians, crossed into Austria during the morning of November 8, by which time all but a few remaining pockets of resistance in the capital had been overcome by superior force. In Budapest, in the industrial area of Csepel, an island in the Danube, the only significant armed resistance continued until November 13. Then it was ruthlessly snuffed out. Eventually an estimated 25,000 Hungarians and several thousand Russians and pro-Russian Hungarians were killed.

Throughout the city, thousands of structures were damaged. The Czech, British, French and Egyptian legations, and hundreds of buildings, including the South railway station in Buda, were completely destroyed. Many compared the destruction to that wrought by the Russians in ousting the Germans from Budapest during the Second World War.

On November 10 the Hungarian President, Istvan Dobi, declared that all those suspected of murder, arson or looting would be summarily executed within 24 hours of their apprehension. Deportation to Siberia of many young people involved in the uprising was reported underway by November 13. Thereafter, the numbers of those attempting to flee the country increased sharply. Eventually some 200,000 Hungarian refugees made their way to Western Europe.

Gadenus father and son, hearing tales from fellow refugees of the blood bath which took place in Budapest after they had been spirited away, were almost thankful to the NKVD. Whatever resentment they felt about the peremptory manner in which they were forced to leave and the new role they were required to assume, was dissipated when, about four weeks after they arrived in a refugee camp near Vienna, they were contacted by the NKVD and given considerable sums of cash in U.S. dollars. By that time their applications for admission to the United States and Canada were being considered by the immigration authorities of those two countries, both of which had adopted emergency procedures to speed up the admission of Hungarian refugees.

Early in 1957 the Gadenus family was informed that they would be admitted to Canada under the terms of a scheme dispensing with the usual screening procedures, in order to facilitate the enormous difficulties of transporting, accommodating, training and placing the tens of thousands of immigrants involved.

Shortly before they were to leave, they were visited by a second

NKVD agent. Unlike the man who had handed them money, the second man had an air of authority about him. He introduced himself as Hans.

"Our information, through our contacts with the Canadian immigration office, is that you are likely to end up in the industrial area of Canada — Ontario. Ernö's skills as a watchmaker will likely mean he will be placed in some industry where they can be used. You Péter — we want you to get further academic training, after the Canadian authorities teach you English. You should go to university. It will take time, but we are in no hurry. You will need more money."

He handed Ernö Gadenus an envelope. When Ernö counted it, the sum was thirty thousand dollars in one thousand U.S. dollar notes. Together with what they had received earlier it made nearly forty thousand dollars — a tidy sum.

"But how can I get this into Canada? They will want to know how I got it."

"In Canada they do not have currency controls."

"No currency controls?"

For as long as Ernö Gadenus could remember, he had lived under currency controls — before World War II, under Admiral Horthy, under the Nazis and in post-war Hungary.

"No controls?"

"No controls. There are customs checks but only for things like cigarettes and liquor or if one purchases very expensive items outside the country, like cameras. In your case I doubt there will even be a customs check since you are being admitted as refugees. All the paper work will be done in advance. They probably will only count heads."

Ernö shook his head in disbelief. What kind of a country were they going to?

"What will I do with the money?"

"Spend it."

"Spend it?"

"Yes. The Canadian authorities will provide you with help of all kinds — even money, perhaps low-interest loans, accommodation, training, and initially probably even food and clothing. Take it. Take anything they offer. In time you will need money to establish yourselves in the community. Use the money you have been given for that purpose. Perhaps you can increase it, after all it is a capitalist country."

The man calling himself Hans smiled. Although probably a Russian or possibly a Ukranian, Ernö Gadenus thought the man looked Austrian. His face was deeply sunburned. He was not tall but he was strongly built with a compact, wiry body. Only the man's eyes suggested that he might have Slavic ancestors. They were jet black and somewhat slanted. Perhaps some ancestor had been among those tough horsemen who had swept across the steppes from Asia, centuries ago. Gadenus' day-dreaming was interrupted by Hans' voice.

"It is most important that you never contact the Soviet Embassy in Canada. The Residentura in Ottawa must never be approached by either of you. You understand?"

They nodded mutely.

"If you wish to communicate with us the following will be the procedure."

Péter Gadenus shifted nervously in his seat.

"You will send a postcard to either of these addresses."

He handed them a slip of paper with the addresses typed on it.

"They are in the United States."

"Yes. As you will note, the person being addressed is a woman. Simply include in the text of the message your address and, when you have one, your telephone number. The message can be about anything banal — the weather, your health, your garden. Sign the card with either of your given names — Ernö or Péter. You will be contacted."

Ernö Gadenus spoke.

"May we keep the paper?"

"No. Memorize the addresses. Not hard. Both are post office boxes, one in New York City and one in San Francisco. The woman's name, Mary Smith, should not be difficult to remember."

The man paused. His sun-burned face expressionless.

"Is that clear?"

"Yes," Ernö replied.

"Your first task will be to establish yourselves. Gain respectability in the community. Take out Canadian citizenship as soon as you can. Péter, you must get an education and a job. Something which will bring you into the government or politics — federal politics. It is no use wasting time on provincial politics — that will be of little use to us. Use the money for that purpose. If you need more it will be provided."

The man calling himself Hans stopped speaking. He sat for some time, the index finger of his right hand tapping the table in front of him. He stared from father to son.

"As you both will appreciate we are investing a good deal of money and effort in you. Do not make the mistake of thinking that once you are in Canada you can forget us. If we do not hear from you we will assume that you are trying to avoid your obligations to us. That would not be a healthy thing for either of you to attempt.

We would find you eventually. It would take time, that is all. Do you both understand?"

Ernö cleared his throat as if to say something. Hans looked at him.

"Well?"

"Yes. We understand."

"Good. Be sure you remember what I said. A bad memory in such matters could be fatal."

* * * * * * * * * * * * * * * * * * *

George McCain brought Brad the first reports from the surveillance squad.

"Boy, the Prime Minister sure hit the nail on the head. The guy's a real billy-goat. He has them in his apartment morning, noon and night. Different girls. So far nothing to link him to anything to do with espionage. When they installed the microphones, they had a quick look around but they were in too much of a hurry to do a thorough job. We would need a clear seven or eight hours to do a proper search — ideally, a whole day."

"Anything from the telephone?"

"Nope. He seldom uses it except to call his mother in Kitchener and to summon his various girl-friends. His mail has been equally unexceptional. Mostly bills. One interesting post-card from Budapest. The crypto boys are having a good look at it."

Several days passed with little to show for the considerable resources and the tremendous effort going into the surveillance coverage of Peter Gustav Gadenus. Review of the original papers which established the Gadenus family in Canada as political refugees revealed at least one report which had not been fully investigated due no doubt to the flood of applications being handled at the time. The report suggested that Gadenus senior may have sought to conceal membership in the Hungarian Communist Party executive. In itself, membership in the party was not a very serious matter since many of those who fled Hungary at the time were party members — unless they had been, they could not have been employed. Membership in the executive was another thing. There was on file a report by another refugee alleging that Gadenus had been a senior party functionary with affiliations with the Hungarian secret police. The report was dismissed at the time as being the comments of someone who had a grudge against Gadenus — he claimed that Gadenus owed him a considerable sum of money, but he was unable to substantiate either claim.

After the first week of surveillance there was little about the life of Peter Gustav Gadenus which was not known to the Security Service. His mail was perlustrated, his telephone and telegraphic communications were intercepted, his apartment was laced with electronic eavesdropping devices, he was photographed with powerful telephoto lenses, clothed, in the nude and in various compromising stances with his stable of girl-friends. However, none of this brought the Security Service any closer to resolving their doubts about him.

"Damn it. He's clean. There isn't one shred of evidence to suggest he is a spy."

"What about the post-card from Hungary?"

"Nothing. The message is in Hungarian. Apparently harmless. Some female relative with whom he evidently has kept up a correspondence. The crypto boys found nothing. There were no micro-dots. There was nothing hidden in the writing or in the paper. Zilch."

"Discouraging, after all the work we've put into it."

"There is one encouraging fact."

"What?"

"He has told his mother he will visit her this weekend. If he does, we'll move a team in as soon as the Watcher Service cars report him fifty kilometres out of town. A full scale Level Two search."

"Good. Keep me in the picture George. How is it going with Orion?"

"Slowly. Patricia Haley has come down with the flu. Lepreau is helping the first team. They have decided to go back to the beginning — trying to fill in holes here and there. Time consuming and frustrating, since Orion doesn't like going over what he has already said."

As Saturday dawned, Brad awoke early to the sickening realization that the muted noises of traffic, which usually were loud even on weekends in Marianne's eleventh floor apartment, were due to falling snow. It looked as if several inches had fallen overnight. Brad cursed. It would be just their luck if Gadenus decided to cancel his trip. By eight o'clock, the snow had almost stopped and shafts of sunlight came through the clouds. Maybe they would be lucky, for once. By ten o'clock, after a telephone call from George McCain, he knew they were.

"He's gone. We thought it might be off until he called his mother to say he might be late due to bad driving conditions. At one point she urged him not to attempt the journey if the driving was dangerous. Thank God, he paid no attention to her."

The Ottawa surveillance teams encountered no difficulty in following Péter Gadenus to the eastern outskirts of Toronto, where they turned him over to teams from the Toronto area. From Ottawa to Toronto, Gadenus took Highway 7 to Peterborough where he turned south to Highway 401. He stopped once for gas, coffee and a sandwich. He continued west on 401, taking the first exit to Kitchener. The Toronto team were surprised when their quarry stopped at a cross-roads five blocks from his destination.

"What the hell is he up to? We better report to the back-up car he's made an unscheduled stop."

"Okay."

"Looks as if he's headed for the post box on the corner."

The man beside the driver spoke quietly into the microphone in his hand, giving their location and the precise location of the post box into which Gadenus dropped what appeared to be a letter.

"Damn. That is going to be problem. A job for the Toronto special squad. Saturday afternoon. Probably the last pick-up was at 10 a.m. and the next one won't be until 10 a.m. tomorrow. I'll check with the back-up team."

He spoke briefly into the microphone, listening to the other half of the conversation over the small earphone set into the shank of the glasses he was wearing.

"Yeah, we're in luck. Next pick-up is at 10 a.m. They are going to call headquarters, Toronto. The decision will be theirs. If they decide to go for it, I guess the special squad will come down from Ottawa tonight."

From the postbox they followed Gadenus to his mother's house, where he parked his car in the asphalt driveway running up to a small garage attached to the house. Gadenus removed a suitcase from the trunk of his car and entered the house by the back door.

In the meantime, for Brad Randall, it was one of the longest Saturday afternoons he had ever spent. Following George McCain's telephone call about ten in the morning informing him that the search was underway, he decided to stay near the telephone in Marianne Carrière's apartment. He received a further call at one o'clock merely to say that the search was in full swing and had not turned up anything the least bit suspicious. By four o'clock, approximately the same time as the Toronto team watched Gadenus make the mail drop, he had heard nothing more and was on the point of calling George McCain, when McCain called him.

"They're still hard at it. Nothing, Brad. Absolutely nothing. I find it hard to believe he is clean. But we can't go much further today. It will be dark soon and the boys would have to turn the lights on and run the risk of someone spotting them. I suggest we call the team off until tomorrow. We'll post an all night sentry so that we don't have to remove the equipment."

Brad accepted George McCain's advice with reluctance. He

turned away from the telephone and stumbled into the arms of Marianne.

"I have a strange feeling the world will not end overnight," she said. "Now, I'm hungry and you're buying dinner."

He smiled and kissed her knowing that the evening would be much more enjoyable than the day had been. But the business of the day had one more wrinkle to present. As Brad and Marianne returned to her apartment after dinner, the telephone was ringing. Marianne answered.

"Yes. He's here, George. Hold on."

"For you. George McCain."

"Yes, George?"

"Decisions, decisions. Sorry to bother you, Brad. Message from Toronto. They need an answer tonight. I think you will want to read the telex."

"Okay. I'll be there as soon as I can."

At the office, Brad placed the telex message on his desk. He stood up and walked back and forth.

"In a nutshell, they're proposing we steal the postbox and replace it with an identical box, using for the purpose the old post office van we sometimes employ for surveillance work in the Toronto area — the one fitted with video equipment. The contents of that box — including the Gadenus letter if we can identify it — would be re-posted elsewhere, after we examine the letter we're interested in."

"That's the way I read it."

"Ingenious. Certainly unorthodox. However, I simply am not prepared to authorize such an operation on my own hook. Given all the flack the Security Service has received in recent years, at the very least, I would want ministerial approval. Without such authority I would be placing those involved at risk. The problem is that this entire case is very unusual — I've ended up as a glorified case officer and the Prime Minister is the responsible Minister."

Brad paused. George McCain remained silent.

"In the circumstances, I would have to ask her agreement. How the hell can I do that when I can't offer her proof positive that Gadenus is a Russian spy? I have nothing to say at this point. What's more, I won't have anything unless the second team come up with something tomorrow. Even then the proof will have to be sufficiently convincing to act upon. Do you agree?"

George McCain grunted.

"Yes, I agree."

"Okay. Send a reply to Toronto saying I am not willing to approve such an operation. Add the reasons for my decision. Also make it perfectly clear that no attempt of any kind — emphasize *any* — is to be made to intercept Gadenus' letter. I don't want them even to ask the local "postie", who clears the box, to let them have a quick look at the contents — something their zeal might lead them to contemplate."

George McCain grinned.

"I read you loud and clear. I will ask for an acknowledgement by telex."

"It's too bad, but we'll just have to forget Gadenus' letter. I see no alternative. Okay?"

"I understand."

"I'll be spending the night at Marianne's apartment. You can get me there if you need me — but please try not to need me."

Sunday passed as tediously as Saturday had done. Brad decided once again to wait out the hours with Marianne. At least with her he could relish the memory of their previous night's lovemaking. By two o'clock he was pacing the floor.

"What you need, Brad, is a drink."

"Thanks. That's exactly what I need. This damn business. Why in hell's name didn't I become a civil servant — unionized, five days a week, nine to five?"

Brad had hardly taken a sip of the drink he poured himself when the telephone rang. He answered before the bell could sound the second time.

"Hello?"

"George here. We've hit the jack-pot."

Brad expelled his breath noisily. He could not disguise his relief and his excitement.

"Jesus. Are you sure?"

"No question. Documentary proof. Perhaps you had better come to headquarters. The fellows are on their way here now. Difficult to say much on the telephone."

"Okay. I'll be there in fifteen minutes."

When Brad got to his office, George McCain and the two senior members of the search team were already there. They gave a succinct report. One of the team, using a sophisticated piece of equipment developed to determine what lay beneath floor boards without having to rip them up, noticed a narrow band of grease around a drain pipe in the bathroom where he was working. Closer examination showed that grease had been applied to the screw threads at an elbow joint near the ceiling. His curiosity aroused, he consulted the blueprints of the alterations made to the old building when it had been converted to apartments, which the Security Service obtained for the search. The drawings showed the pipe no longer was in use.

Using a chain wrench, he unscrewed an eighteen inch length of the pipe which was fitted to rest on a metal collar allowing about three inches of clearance. The screw threads of the metal collar were smoothly ground to allow the pipe to be easily removed. The length of pipe was discovered to have a skilfully fitted wooden bottom. Inside was a dry container measuring 16 inches long and 7½ inches in diameter. They found a number of documents in the container, neatly wrapped in a thick plastic cover. Included among the papers were photocopies of two Cabinet documents, copies of various Cabinet Decisions, a draft paper intended for consideration by the Cabinet Committee on Priorities and Planning and numerous handwritten notes. The collection included a number of documents which appeared to be unclassified. In all there were about thirty pieces of paper.

"Where are the documents now?"

"Still in Gadenus' apartment. They are being photographed and they will be replaced exactly as they were found — precisely in the order they were discovered. Incidentally, we are reasonably certain there was no booby-trap — Gadenus probably saw no need to set one up. It will take the boys at least another two hours before they can finish up and remove all trace of their presence. Because we won't get another crack at the documents we are taking the precaution of photographing them twice. We'd look pretty silly if the negatives were no good and we ended up without any proof to offer."

"You have seen the documents. You are sure they are incriminating?"

The younger of the two team members replied.

"No question, Sir. I made a note of the more important items. As you will see, the Cabinet documents are numbered, and include dates, subject and security classification. Same for the Cabinet Decision and the draft document for the CCPP."

He handed Brad his notes. Brad read them carefully.

"Thanks. It seems we have enough to make a good case. Good work. My congratulations to your colleagues and especially to the man who discovered the hidden container."

"Edwards, Sir. His name is Edwards. Corporal Edwards. He's had plenty of experience. Been at it fourteen years."

"George, can you make a note of his name. Okay, not much more we can do until the photography is finished and the prints developed. When will that be?"

"Not until much later tonight, Sir."

"Okay. Can we agree to meet here tomorrow at nine? That won't give you a hell of a lot of time for your beauty rest but it will give you some. If the evidence is as damaging as it seems now, I'll try to see the Prime Minister in the late morning. When is Gadenus expected to return?"

George McCain answered.

"We aren't certain. The surveillance team covering him in

Kitchener reported an hour ago that he is still there. We did our planning on the premise that since he drove down, he will drive back. That should give us six or seven hours notice — and we can also arrange a few delays for traffic infractions if we have to."

"Okay. Until tomorrow then."

Five

When Brad arrived at his office, George McCain and the two members of the search team with whom they had discussed the material discovered in Péter Gadenus' apartment on Saturday afternoon, already were there. Spread on the small conference table were about twenty photographs. Shortly after Brad appeared they were joined by Murray Saunders, head of Q section — special photography.

"Sorry to be late. We've been working on the photographs of the handwritten notes. As George may have told you, the first set of negatives turned out to be impossible to print. Something wrong with the resolution and the lighting. Thank God they decided to take two shots of everything. The second set are better but it was necessary to play around with them quite a bit to get a readable text. This is about the best we can hope for."

He placed eight enlargements, measuring 8 inches by 11 inches, on the table with the other photographs. Brad and George McCain examined them.

"Legible as far as I'm concerned. Bit indistinct at the edges. Thank God he wrote them in English and not Hungarian. Have you analyzed them yet?"

"No. There hasn't been time for proper analysis, but it seems obvious they are notes about people. Talent spotting notes, I guess. Mostly people he has come in contact with in his work — Members of Parliament, Ministers, staff people. Not surprisingly many of them are about women. One or two seem to concern the wives of Ministers — from the comments it seems clear his knowledge of the ladies is intimate, no doubt obtained at first hand."

Brad returned the photographs he was exmaining.

"What about the sixty-four dollar question? Have we sufficient evidence to satisfy the Prime Minister that Gadenus is what we suspect him of being?"

George McCain replied.

"I don't think there is any doubt on that score. We will have to check with Privy Council Office to be certain these are copies of genuine Cabinet documents and Cabinet decisions. I will be very surprised if they are not. That being the case, I think we have enough to convince the Prime Minister and others that Gadenus has been carrying out espionage. The problem then will be to decide what can and should be done next."

Brad looked at George McCain.

"You're right, George. Assuming she is convinced by the evidence, the Prime Minister's first question will be, 'What do you recommend?' To some extent the answer to that depends upon a legal opinion — can he be arrested under the Official Secrets Act on the basis of the evidence we have? Based upon past experience, I suspect the answer will be no. Unfortunately, because of the peculiar nature of the case and Orion's central role, I am not able to seek an opinion from the Justice Department before speaking to the Prime Minister. There is also the question of whether from our standpoint we think the laying of charges under the Official Secrets Act is the best course to recommend. There are good arguments for not doing so."

George McCain cleared his throat.

"So far all we've got are copies of classified documents found in Gadenus' apartment. Nothing more. We can't even prove that he copied them and, if he's smart, he will refuse to say anything, insist on a lawyer and sit back and let the Crown try to prove he's been engaged in espionage. Something it will be almost impossible to prove in court. At best we might get him for possession of classified documents to which he is not entitled — as much an indictment of the system as it is an indictment of Gadenus. Unless a judge is willing to agree to a large bail there is nothing to prevent him from skipping the country. In the circumstances, I can't see a judge agreeing to fix bail, at least not in an amount sufficient to deter him."

"I agree. Okay. I assume the Special Analysis Group will be brought into the picture. I would like to have an analysis of the material before I see the Prime Minister. In the meantime, I want the authenticity of the documents checked out and Gadenus kept under constant surveillance. The interrogation teams should be brought into the picture since this development could have an important bearing on our continued interrogation of Orion. Depending on what more we find out about Gadenus, it also could have some bearing on the inquiries which the Americans and the British are carrying out. However, I do not want them informed of this latest development until I have spoken to the Prime Minister."

George McCain stayed behind when the others left. He filled Brad in on the return of Gadenus to his apartment the previous evening.

"He returned about ten. Nothing unusual on the return journey. He came back by Highway 401, turning north onto Highway 31 at Morrisburg. He stopped only for coffee and to fill up with gas.

They saw him into his apartment building and the audio surveillance confirmed he spent the night there — with a girl-friend. He called her about ten minutes after getting back. He sure has a one-track mind. He's at his office now and we have him under surveillance there — but it's difficult to maintain it in a Minister's office. We just have to hope for the best."

"Okay, George. Thank you."

As McCain left, Brad reflected that without him life would be difficult — very difficult. The man was indefatigable. It was late that evening before Brad could arrange a meeting with the Prime Minister. She had been in Vancouver giving a speech to a fund-raising dinner for the party. It was arranged for her to see Brad as soon as she returned, at her residence on Sussex Drive.

"Well, Mr. Randall?"

She looked tired and clearly was not in a good humour. Brad wondered if it might not have been wiser to have waited until morning before tackling her. Unfortunately, the timing of the meeting was not something he controlled — he was in the hands of her appointments secretary, whose friendship he had assiduously cultivated over a period of time. By arranging a meeting so promptly, obviously she was trying to do him a favour.

"Sorry to bother you at this hour, Prime Minister. There has been a development in the Gadenus case which requires a Ministerial decision."

"Gadenus? Oh, yes, The billy goat?"

"Yes. As you will recall, we have had him under close surveillance. We now have documentary evidence which strongly suggests he is involved in espionage."

The Prime Minsiter remained silent. Brad quickly sketched in the events which led to the discovery of Cabinet and other documents in Gadenus' apartment.

"Have you the photographs with you?"

"Yes. I brought copies of everything we found."

Opening his briefcase, Brad handed her the documents. She placed them on the desk at which she was sitting. Adjusting the table lamp to throw a better light, she examined them one by one carefully. Brad noted with admiration that she had no need of reading glasses.

"Interesting. What do you make of these handwritten notes, which, I am glad you had typed? He has terrible writing."

"They are character sketches of various people with whom he has come in contact in his job. The information could be useful to someone interested in drawing up lists of possible future recruits. Some of the information could be the basis for attempted blackmail."

"So I notice. Some of my colleagues' wives would not be

flattered I think by Mr. Gadenus' comments about them. He obviously has charms of one kind or another."

For the first time she permitted herself a smile.

"What do you recommend?"

"We would like to pick him up for questioning. Even if there
are considered to be sufficient legal grounds to press charges under
the Official Secrets Act we feel we might get further by seeking his
co-operation."

"Do you have a legal opinion?"

"No, Prime Minister. Given the peculiar nature of the case and
its close relationship to our continuing investigation of Orion, I felt
I should have your approval before approaching the Justice
department."

"What if the Justice officials are of the opinion a successful
conviction could be obtained?"

"I think our preference would still be to get him to co-operate.
Once charges are laid, that would be difficult if not impossible to
achieve. There are other considerations. Given past experience
with the Official Secrets Act I assume there would be objections to
attempting to hold a trial 'in camera'. That being so, the case would
have to become public, including presumably the kind of material
contained in the handwritten notes. The press would love it, but I
doubt those involved would be very happy. More important from
our standpoint, the publicity might have some effect upon our
continuing investigation of Orion."

"You want me to agree that Gadenus should be questioned
unofficially, as it were?"

"Yes, Prime Minister. I also would like your agreement to our
seeking an opinion from Justice about the legal aspects of the
problem."

The Prime Minister handed back the papers. She rose, smooth-
ing her skirt.

"Very well, Mr. Randall. You have my approval."

"One further thing, Prime Minister. I wonder if you would
mind initialling the memorandum covering the documents."

Brad handed her the memorandum. Leaning across the desk
she placed her initials on the top right hand corner with the date.
She returned the paper to Brad.

"For posterity, no doubt?"

He noted, with relief, that the words were said mischievously,
but decided that silence was the better part of valour and withdrew.

Brad set in motion the arrangements to question Gadenus in
his apartment the next morning at 8 a.m., at least an hour before he
normally went to his office in the Houses of Parliament. No other

action was to be taken until an opinion was forthcoming from the Justice department. When Justice officials were told the story (although nothing about Orion), they responded quickly, especially when they learned of the Prime Minister's personal involvement. The initial legal opinion was that while there was a *prima facie* case against Gadenus it was unlikely the photographs of the documents taken by the Security Service would be considered as admissible evidence in court.

"I know the opinion is tentative and preliminary. However, I doubt that it is likely to change much with the passage of time. Time is a scarce commodity for us. Our best bet is to confront Gadenus in the hope that he'll co-operate in return for an offer of immunity. Are Justice aware that we want to take that course?"

"Yes, although I had the impression that they don't much like the idea of offering him immunity."

"Then how the hell do they suggest we get him to confess? Offer him life membership in a Paris brothel?"

George McCain chuckled.

"That might be pretty persuasive with Gadenus. No, Justice didn't offer suggestions on that score. They didn't advise against an offer of immunity — they just weren't enthusiastic."

Brad snorted impatiently.

"Christ. Where does that leave us?"

"Just about where we've always been — damned if we do and damned if we don't."

"Okay. Let's move in on Gadenus tomorrow morning. Anything in the surveillance reports against doing so?"

"No. He hasn't done anything unusual in the last forty-eight hours. Gone to work in the morning. Screwed twice — once during his lunch hour. Took in a movie. Phoned his mother and a couple of girl-friends. The only mail he's had have been bills. He sent a postcard to an address in Hungary — there wasn't anything special about it — no hidden messages, microdots or codes we could discover."

"Who's going to do the interrogation?"

"I thought I would run it using Kurt Oppler as the lead man. He speaks German and has a knowledge of Hungarian. He had a Hungarian grandmother. He's had experience. He was the interrogator in the Janitor case. Did a good job. He does his homework. We can use Bill Lewis as the number two man. He has a nice flexibility that will make him a good partner to Oppler."

The following morning was wet and windy. The kind of day which encourages people to sleep late. Péter Gadenus was no exception. When he answered the door to George McCain's insistent ringing of the bell, he was still in his pyjamas, obviously half asleep. He peered at his visitors.

"Yes? What do you want?"

McCain pushed his identification badge through the door and said in a quiet voice.

"We're RCMP officers. We would like to talk to you."

He was startled. A look of fear came across his face. He made as if to close the door. George McCain placed his hand on the door.

"What do you want?"

"If you will let us in we will explain, unless, of course, you would like all your neighbours to take part in the conversation."

There was a sound of a door shutting on the floor above and footsteps on the stairway. Reluctantly, Gadenus opened the door wider to admit them. When they were inside George McCain shut the door behind him.

"I apologize for the early hour but we wished to talk to you before you went to your office."

"Who are you? What do you want? I haven't done anything."

"Here is my identification, which I showed you earlier. Here is the identification of my colleague. Perhaps you would like to dress and we can talk here."

George McCain waved in the direction of the living room on their right. Gadenus did not reply but headed to the back of the apartment with McCain on his heels. As McCain watched, Gadenus pulled on a pair of blue jeans and a sweater. His hair was still dishevelled, his eyes bleary.

"I gotta have some coffee. You want some?"

"No thanks. We have had some earlier."

George McCain watched as he made coffee and poured himself a cup. When they re-joined Kurt Oppler in the front room Gadenus took a sip. His hand shook as he brought the cup to his lips.

"What's this all about? Have I parked in the wrong place again on the Hill?"

"It's a bit more serious than a parking infraction, Mr. Gadenus. We have reason to believe that you are engaged in espionage."

The blood drained from Gadenus' face and he said something which George McCain didn't understand. He glanced at Kurt Oppler. The latter nodded slightly. McCain took that to mean he had understood — probably some Hungarian expression.

"What are you talking about?"

"We would not make such an accusation without good reason, Mr. Gadenus."

"I want to call a lawyer. I know my rights."

"You are perfectly at liberty to do so. But I think you had

better hear what we have to say before you take any hasty steps."

"Are you arresting me?"

"No, Mr. Gadenus. We do not have a warrant for your arrest but we can get one if that is necessary. We hope that it won't be necessary. We know of your activities."

"What activities? Your bluffing."

"No, Mr. Gadenus. We are not bluffing. I will show you what I mean. Come with me."

George McCain moved towards the bathroom at the rear of the apartment. Gadenus followed with Kurt Oppler taking up the rear in the narrow corridor. When they were in the bathroom McCain pointed to the drain pipe.

"We know about your hiding place."

As McCain moved a chair under the pipe where it fitted into an elbow joint near the ceiling, he caught an expression on Gadenus' face which made him uneasy — a sly, triumphant look. What the hell did it mean? George McCain thought he knew. If he was right he was going to have to do some pretty fancy footwork to outwit the bastard. He unscrewed the length of pipe and lowered it carefully. The container was empty! George McCain kept all expression from his face. He caught the look of dismay on Kurt Oppler's face and was glad that Gadenus had his back to Oppler. Years of playing poker every Thursday night with a collection of some of the toughest poker players in Ottawa had prepared George McCain for this moment.

"Okay, Gadenus, the game's up. You've cleared this but not before we photographed the contents — including Cabinet Decision 374-R."

George McCain was glad to see a flicker of doubt replace the look of self-confidence which had been on Gadenus' face as he removed the section of empty pipe.

"What are you talking about? A piece of empty pipe. So what?"

"Not simply a piece of empty pipe, Gadenus. A secret hiding place for the documents you have been stealing from your Minister's office — documents which you recently attempted to mail in the House of Commons post office. Documents which we photographed when they were still here and from which we obtained several excellent finger prints — including prints which have been identified as yours. Don't think that we haven't been following your every move. The documents in question are documents to which you are not permitted access — documents you sent to your masters."

George McCain held his breath. Had he overplayed his hand? It didn't amount to more than a pair of nines. There were no usable fingerprints. No mail had been intercepted in the Commons post office. The change of expression told him what he wanted to know. The bluff had worked. Gadenus' eyes took on a hunted look. George McCain pressed his advantage.

"Look, Gadenus, we've got enough on you to put you behind bars for a long time. I can pick you up now and have a warrant for your arrest within the hour or you can play it our way."

"What do you mean?"

"I mean that if you co-operate with us there need be no charges — no prison sentence."

"How do I know you will keep your word?"

"You don't. But then you are hardly in a position to doubt us. We have the goods on you. As you can imagine, we have had a great deal of experience — we have a reputation to uphold. If we promise no charges will be laid against you, we will see the promise is kept."

Gadenus shifted uneasily from one foot to the other. His small eyes swivelled from McCain to Oppler.

George McCain fought to keep the relief he felt from showing on his face. He could feel the sweat under his arms. Christ, that had been close. What the hell had gone wrong? How had Gadenus emptied the pipe without their knowing? He thought he knew the answer and had gambled on being right. Thank God he remembered the comment in the surveillance teams' reports that Gadenus always carried a briefcase to and from work. The day after Gadenus' return from Kitchener he recalled the surveillance reports indicated that Gadenus, carrying his briefcase, had gone first to the Centre Block of the parliament buildings instead of going directly to his office in the West Block. At the time, McCain had wondered why Gadenus had varied his routine. Fortuitously, the answer came to him when the pipe was found empty. Gadenus had mailed the documents in the Centre Block post office, no doubt to some post office box in the National Capital area, which would be serviced by the KGB. Simple, safe and devilishly clever. George McCain thanked his lucky stars that Gadenus was ignorant of the fact that their surveillance was not allowed to carry into the parliament buildings — for this they were obliged to depend upon occasional co-operation by members of the House of Commons security staff.

"We want you to come with us to the Skyline Hotel. We have reserved a suite there where we can talk in a more relaxed and secure atmosphere. Among other things it will be safer for you."

Gadenus looked sullen.

"What do you mean?"

"Well, in accepting your co-operation we also accept responsibility for protecting you."

A startled look appeared on Gadenus' face.

"Protect me? You mean against the KGB?"

George McCain nearly let out a whoop of joy. The silly bugger. He was properly hooked now. It was clear they were not dealing with a professional.

"Yes, Péter. That is exactly what I mean. I suggest we go immediately to the Skyline. We'll wait while you shave and finish dressing. We can have breakfast there."

Kurt Oppler looked at McCain with a grin as Gadenus started to run water in the wash basin.

"Okay, Kurt you stay with him."

Six

The suite in the Skyline Hotel was on one of the uppermost floors, overlooking the Ottawa River to the west. It was one of George McCain's favourite views of the river, the ancient route taken by voyageurs seeking to trade their wares for valuable fur pelts. Even today with the virgin stands of timber stripped from its banks and replaced by ugly concrete and steel buildings it reeked of romance. As the RCMP doctor went over Péter Gadenus with stethoscope and prying fingers, it was obvious the magnificent view through the huge plate glass windows was lost on Gadenus — his vision was inward.

"What the hell is this. I don't need a doctor. There's nothing wrong with me."

Gadenus stood before the doctor who was seated on a straight backed chair, facing him. George McCain could see how the man had earned the sobriquet "Stallion".

"All right. You can put your clothes on."

Gadenus dressed with bad grace.

"You never said anything about a doctor."

George McCain looked at him. He might not be a professional in one sense of the word but he was going to be a nuisance. A barrack-room lawyer if he had ever seen one.

"No. We didn't mention a medical examination. It is routine. We are responsible for you. We simply want to be sure that you're healthy before we start questioning you. If you have some medical condition calling for medication or special care we would want to know so that we can take account of it while you are in our custody."

"Covering your asses."

"Yes, and yours too."

The doctor finished re-packing his bag and snapped it shut.

"As far as I'm concerned he has clean bill of health. I'll send my written report, as usual."

It was clear the earlier shock of being confronted, without warning, by George McCain and Kurt Oppler was beginning to wear off. Oppler, his fellow-interrogator, Bill Lewis, and the two technicians were going to have their hands full.

"Okay. I'll leave you. Between now and lunch time, I'll see

about arranging the country house for tonight and the next few days. Call me if you need anything. Péter, the sooner you answer the questions the sooner we can all finish this thing."

"Why the hell should I?"

"It's up to you. If you don't want to co-operate we will proceed to lay charges under the Official Secrets Act."

Gadenus didn't make any reply but sat in the seat indicated to him by Kurt Oppler, in front of a Uher tape recorder set on the table before him. One of the technicians started the machine going. The reels began to turn silently. George McCain left the room.

"Okay, Péter. Let's take it slowly from the beginning. Your name, where were you born and when."

"You know that."

"We want it for the record. In your words."

Kurt Oppler pointed to the tape recorder. Gadenus looked as if he would argue and then shrugged his shoulders.

"My name is Péter Gustav Gadenus. Born October 3rd, 1937, in Dunaharaszti."

"Spell it."

"What?"

"The name of the town."

"It's near Budapest. South."

"Fine, but spell it."

'D-U-N-A-H-A-R-A-S-Z-T-I."

"Who was your father?"

"Ernö Gadenus."

"Any other names?"

"Yes, Ferencz."

"Spell it."

"Frank in Canada, F-E-R-E-N-C-Z."

"Your mother's name . . . ."

It proved to be slow work — hour after hour which was not helped by his attitude. Gradually the story of his early years in school and later, built up. By lunch time they had been through his initial recruitment by the KGB and the despatch of the Gadenus family in the guise of refugees to Austria and subsequently to Canada. By the time George McCain returned, about three o'clock in the afternoon, they had begun to get into the arrangements the KGB made to keep him on a string during the years of his apprenticeship — names of contacts, places and frequency of meetings.

"We're only starting to get into tradecraft. It's like pulling teeth. He's a difficult son of a bitch. It's hard work. I'd like to suggest we pack it in pretty soon. Are we decided upon the country house for tonight?"

"I leave that for you and Bill to decide. If you think you've made enough headway, it's free and ready for you."

"We've enough to make it worth continuing. There's no way he can back out now. I think we have a sufficient body of material for the next stages. If he attempts to contradict himself, he'll find it difficult."

"Good. There is some urgency in relation to the interrogation of Orion. At first blush I'd say this seems to establish Orion's credibility. However, I'm inclined to be cautious until we know a hell of a lot more about Gadenus' current activities and methods of operation."

By four-thirty Kurt Oppler, Bill Lewis and Gadenus were in an unmarked car speeding north on Highway 5 in the direction of the Gatineau Hills. The two technicians were left to pack up the equipment and check out of the hotel.

"Where are we going? I want my clothes and shaver."

Kurt Oppler sitting beside Gadenus in the back seat, answered.

"We are going to a safe house, where we can continue our talk. You will find everything you need there, including a razor and clothing. We have brought you a new wardrobe. We took the sizes from your clothing while you were being given a medical examination."

Péter Gadenus made no answer. He glared at Kurt Oppler and turned his head to look out the window at the passing countryside. Oppler did not explain that one reason he could not be given his personal effects was that at that moment they were being subjected to a minute examination in the RCMP laboratory. His apartment had been painstakingly examined, inch by inch, together with all the contents. Even the tubes of toothpaste and his electric razor were being dissected and analyzed. Nothing was being left to chance. If there was evidence of his espionage trade, it would be found. In fact there was none and by the time they recommenced their questioning of Gadenus, the next morning, Kurt Oppler knew this. He and Bill Lewis were very aware that any additional information about espionage activities would have to be extracted from Gadenus through interrogation.

Perhaps the peaceful atmosphere of the safe house, in a sylvan setting by the edge of Meach Lake, was responsible for the more cooperative mood displayed by Péter Gadenus in the morning. Whatever the reason, Kurt Oppler welcomed it.

"This man you would meet in Europe, Vasili?"

"Yes. Vasili?"

"He was your contact."

"Yes."

"Do you know his full name?"

"I don't understand."

"Did he have other names?"

"I don't know. The only name he gave was Vasili."

"Was he Russian?"

"Oh, yes. Russian. KGB."

"How often did you meet him?"

"Once, twice a year."

"Where?"

"Different places."

"Yes, but where?"

"Paris, Vienna, Madrid. One meeting in Rome. Nice girls there."

Péter Gadenus' face lit up at the memories evoked by this thought.

"Did you pass information to him at these meetings? Documents?"

"No documents. Too dangerous. Vasili was mad when I brought documents. We talked."

"Talked about what?"

"He told me what to look for."

"Did you provide him with information?"

"Yes, about people. People in government — in the office. Sometimes he asked questions about documents I sent."

"You mean secret documents?"

"Yes. Documents taken from the office."

"How did you send those documents?"

"I don't understand."

"How did you send the documents you took from the office? Dead letter box or mail?"

"Oh. Mail to different addresses and sometimes letter boxes."

"Can you remember them?"

"Perhaps. They changed. Vasili would give me new addresses and letter drops."

"How often?"

"I don't understand."

"How often did Vasili change the addresses and locations of the dead letter boxes?"

"Oh, once, twice a year."

"Okay, Péter. We'll take a break. Here is a piece of paper. I want you to write down all the addresses and dead letter boxes you can remember. It would help to have an approximate period when they were in use. Can you do that?"

"I will need some coffee though."

"You can have all the coffee you want. Anything to eat?"

"Cake."

"Okay."

Péter Gadenus was a slow worker on paper but the result when it was finished took Kurt Oppler by surprise — the crabbed handwriting filled two foolscap pages. Oppler got one of the men guarding the outside of the premises to take Gadenus for a walk on the grounds. Meanwhile he and Bill Lewis studied the list.

"His writing is hard to make out. But if he isn't inventing these, there is nothing wrong with his memory. Quite a list. The surveillance boys will drool over the dead letter drops. If he is telling the truth, only a half dozen are still in use, including one on Parliament Hill of all places. I would like this photo-copied and sent in to George McCain as quickly as possible. Most of the addresses appear to be in Europe — poste restante addresses. Our European friends will be interested. Did you notice? Not one address is in England."

Bill Lewis, who was studying the list intently, looked up.

"You're right. I hadn't noticed. Interesting."

When Gadenus returned from outside they were ready to start again.

"Nice place."

"Yes, Péter. We try to make it comfortable for our guests. That list you drew up is helpful. Very helpful. You have a good memory."

"Vasili made me learn it every time. Hard work. He wouldn't let me go until I knew it."

"How often did you use the dead letter boxes?"

"When I had material. Once, twice a month."

"How did you decide whether to send by mail or use the dead letter boxes? Did Vasili instruct you which method of communication to use?"

"Oh, no. I decided. If I had a lot of material, I split it. Some I sent by mail. The rest I put in a dead letter box."

Gadenus used his hands to indicate a heavy volume of material.

"Didn't you think it risky to use the mail for these purposes?"

Gadenus looked at Oppler with a cunning expression.

"Vasili said Canadians pay no attention to mail. True, hein?"

Kurt Oppler ignored the question.

"Who cleared the dead letter boxes?"

"I don't know. The KGB I suppose."

"How did you let the KGB know that you had filled a dead letter box?"

"Postcard."

"To whom?"

"Different addresses. Sometimes to Hungary. I made it seem as if the person I was writing to was a relative."

"What was the method?"

"What do you mean?"

"How would your 'relative' know that you had left material in a box to be picked up?"

"Oh. The letter boxes were numbered. I would include the

number in the message. I would write it out and include the number in it."

"You mean that if you had filled dead letter box number six you would write six, followed by the numeral 6 in brackets immediately after it? Like this?"

Kurt Oppler scribbled quickly on a pad of paper before him. He shoved it along the table to Gadenus. The latter looked at it for a moment.

"Yes. That's how I did it."

"Can you remember the addresses you have used?"

"Perhaps. Not all."

"I want you to write them down after lunch in the same way you wrote out the dead letter box locations and the poste restante addresses you gave us. Can you do that?"

"Yes. I can do that."

"Was Vasili the only controller you had?"

"Yes. No. There was another at first."

"Do you remember his name?"

"I didn't like him. He was big and strong."

"A Russian?"

"No. Bulgarian."

"Name?"

"Dmitri."

"Illich. Dmitri Illich."

"No surname?"

"Hein?"

"Like Gadenus."

"Oh. No. I don't know his real name. Only Dmitri Illich."

"How did you know he was Bulgarian?"

"He told me. He said all Bulgarians are great men. Better than Hungarians."

"Was he KGB?"

"I think so. He said he was a member of the Durzhavna Sigurnost."

"The what?"

"Durzhavna Sigurnost. Bulgarian State Security. He could also have been KGB. Some Hungarian security members also are members of the KGB."

So it went on until Oppler said,

"Okay, Péter. We'll break for lunch. When we've finished I'd like you to write out the list of addresses of convenience — anything you can remember. Even if you can't remember an entire address — an incomplete one would be helpful."

While Péter Gadenus struggled in his difficult handwriting to compile the list of addresses of convenience, Kurt Oppler and Bill Lewis took the opportunity to get some fresh air. They walked slowly along the gravel path which led to the lake, avoiding the lawn which was still heavy with moisture from the storm which had hit the area a few days earlier.

"His story has the ring of truth about it. It will take time to check out the addresses of convenience and the various dead letter drops he has given us. I will be surprised if he has invented the whole thing. He's not a very attractive specimen, but I think he is trying to co-operate. It is quite clear he has been passing a good deal of material, some of it pretty sensitive stuff. Whether or not we are able to check out his story about methods of communication and so on, he unquestionably has acted as a KGB agent for a number of years. To that extent it would appear that Orion has provided us with valid information."

Bill Lewis stopped to select a flat stone from the gravel path which he attempted to "skip" along the calm surface of the lake, a trick which took him back to his childhood.

"I guess you're right, Kurt, but it's going to be pretty difficult to check out much of what Gadenus has told us. Most of the addresses and the drops are out of use. Some of the dead letter boxes may no longer exist."

"I agree, but even confirmation of a couple of those he claims are current would help to establish his credibility. It might even be of operational value. The use of the monument of John A. Macdonald on Parliament Hill is a good one. If I understand Gadenus, the hiding place is under the figure of the woman holding the shield and the flag standard — Britannia, if my memory serves me well."

Bill Lewis snorted.

"The nerve of the buggers. A pretty good dead letter drop though, when you think of it. The area is concealed behind the East Block, quite open to the public, night and day, and not very well lit at night. It could easily be serviced by someone on foot. A KGB woman operative or a KGB wife could do it. At least it shows the KGB have a sense of humour."

"I think we should question him further about the drops he claims may still be in use. I assume the ones he mentioned were designed only for his use. It is difficult to imagine they would be careless enough to attempt multiple use, but one never knows. They have been pretty hard pressed by the surveillance people these past few months. After all, good drops are hard to establish even in the 18,000 square mile area of the National Capital Area in which they are free to roam under the existing rules of the game."

Kurt Oppler kicked a stone from the path into the lake.

"Boy, that list sure points up the difficulties of carrying out any effective surveillance in such a huge area. If, as you suggest, the list concerns only one agent — in this case Gadenus — imagine how many other dead letter drops they have. With that fleet of cars, each one of them a spy factory on wheels with diplomatic immunity, to which must be added the wheeled resources of the other Soviet Bloc missions, the problem is mind-boggling. All they have to do is make a simultaneous and massive use of their transport facilities, fanning out in different directions, together with agents on foot, to swamp our capabilities."

As they turned to face the house, they could see Péter Gadenus emerge in the company of one of the guards.

"Guess we'd better get back to the job."

The two men walked slowly back to the safe house, savouring the smells and sounds of the country.

"Thanks, Péter. You have done a good job."

Gadenus looked pleased. Kurt Oppler could visualize him as a schoolboy being complimented by some teacher — something he imagined did not happen often."

"Péter, we would like to know more about the dead letter drops you listed, particularly the ones which may be still operational."

"Yes?"

Gadenus looked at Oppler.

"Let's take them one by one. The John A. Macdonald statue. Did you use it?"

"I don't understand."

"The statue — the one beside the Senate."

"The old Prime Minister?"

"Yes. Did you use it?"

"No. I never used it."

"Okay. The next on the list. The *Citizen* newspaper dispenser on the west side of the Byward market. Did you use it?"

"No. I never used it."

"How would that work?"

"What?"

"How did it work?. What was the method for leaving material?"

"Oh. I was supposed to fix a magnetic container to the top of the box. Inside, at the back. Up, above the papers. Only for small things. I never used it."

"When were you told about this drop?"

"Last time I met Vasili."

"When?"

"I don't remember the exact date. About seven or eight months ago. In Madrid."

"How did you know when and where to meet Vasili?"

"Postcard."

"Postcard?"

"Yes. I would receive a postcard from a relative in Budapest."

"How was this done?"

"The postcard would contain date and place. My 'relative' would write she was going to some city — Paris, Rome and give the date. I would be there on that date. Such meetings always took place in the main railway station. By the newspaper kiosk, at 1000 hours. If not at that time then at 1500 hours. This procedure would be repeated the next day, if no contact was made on the first day."

"Were you paid?"

A cunning look came across Péter's face.

"Why do you want to know? You will tell the tax department?"

"No, Péter. I promise you we will not tell the tax authorities."

Gadenus looked from one to the other.

"Why do you want to know?"

"It's important to know how you operated. How the KGB operates."

"Okay. I was paid every time I met Vasili. Only once was I not paid. When I met the Bulgarian."

"Dmitri Illich?"

"Yes. He kept the money for himself."

"How much were you paid on those occasions?"

"Hein?"

"How much money did you receive from Vasili?"

Gadenus didn't answer.

"Péter, we're not interested in whether you reported the money in your income tax returns. We want some idea of what they paid you."

"A few thousand."

"Few thousand what? Francs, dollars, pesetas?"

"Dollars, American dollars."

"In cash?"

"Yes, in cash."

"How much, exactly?"

"I don't remember."

"Péter. You are not telling the truth. Twenty thousand?"

Péter Gadenus looked startled and upset.

"No, no, no. Not so much."

"Then how much? Fifteen, ten?"

"Once, fifteen, after a long time of not meeting Vasili. Most times five, ten thousand."

"How many times have you seen Vasili in the past four years?"

"I don't remember."

·   "Come on, Péter. Don't play games. You have told us you met him twice or three times a year. Is that right?"

"Maybe."

"Okay. So in the past four years you may have met Vasili about a dozen times?"

"No. Not so much. Ten times."

"So you probably received about seventy thousand dollars during this time?"

"No. Not so much. Perhaps fifty."

"Okay. You received fifty. From this you paid your travelling expenses and other out of pocket expenses?"

"Out of what?"

"Other expenses. Food, girls."

"Ah, girls. Yes, I paid for them from the money Vasili gave me. Also airline tickets and hotels. Expensive."

He gave them a crooked smile. Kurt Oppler thought to himself that, given the man's reputation, it would not be surprising if quite a chunk of his spending had gone towards girls. The tax-free aspect of the payments meant that they were worth considerably more than their face value and particularly when the exchange rate was taken into account. There seemed no doubt that the KGB had considered him a valuable asset. It was difficult to believe they would be willing to throw him away merely to establish Orion's credibility.

At the end of the second afternoon, Kurt Oppler and Bill Lewis left Gadenus in the care of the guards and the other members of the safe house. Their report to Brad, George McCain and John Merrivale took some time to make. It was comprehensive. When they had finished and the questioning ended, Brad summed it up.

"I would say there is a strong case for thinking Orion's information about Gadenus is genuine. Anyone disagree?"

None of those present expressed dissent.

"That being the case I suggest we intensify our efforts to follow Orion's leads about the other two agents he claims are in the government. God knows there isn't much to go on except Orion's claims to have seen reports which could only have come from External Affairs. That could mean in Ottawa or somewhere abroad. Like looking for a needle in a haystack. To complicate matters, what little he has told us in the last few days — incidentally, during the same time that you have been interrogating Gadenus — doesn't rule out the possibility that the source is technical rather than human. Perhaps some new, sophisticated piece of equipment in one of our Embassies which the 'sweepers' haven't latched onto. I'll have to tell the Prime Minister. She's not going to like it, but she would like it even less if I didn't keep her informed. Okay, George, let's get the two teams working on it. Lepreau and Patricia Haley have been particularly successful. If they can stand it, perhaps they can be given the lion's share of the work — at least initially."

Seven

As Brad's car pulled up before the west door of the Centre Block he cursed. He was late for his appointment with the Prime Minister. Something he had so far managed to avoid. She was notoriously punctilious herself and could not tolerate unpunctuality in others, a fact Brad was very much aware of, as he was ushered into her office. She sat at her desk, immersed in the papers before her. She didn't look up when he entered, and left him standing silently until she turned her attention to him.

"Ah, Mr. Randall. You are late."

She didn't ask why, but the interrogatory tone of her voice was obvious.

"Sorry, Prime Minister. My car was held up by a fire. The roads were blocked off to the Overbrook bridge."

She looked at him steadily, expressionless. To Brad's relief a slow smile curled her lips.

"A fire?"

"Yes, Prime Minister. At the corner of the River Road and Rideau. It appeared to be one of the gas stations."

"I am sorry to hear it. I should have known that the head of the Security Service would have a good cover story. You asked to see me?"

"Yes, Prime Minister. There have been developments in the Orion case. I thought you would wish to know of them."

"Go ahead."

For the next forty minutes Brad gave her an account of Péter Gadenus' interrogation, the implications in terms of Orion's credibility and the suggestion, from Orion's continuing interrogation, that someone in the Department of External Affairs might be a spy.

"Do you think it possible, Mr. Randall?"

"I don't know. As I indicated all that Orion has told us so far leaves it uncertain that we are, in fact, dealing with a human source. It could just as well be a technical source."

"Technical source?"

"A microphone or some similar technical device for intercepting telegraphic traffic between Ottawa and one of our diplomatic missions — presumably in Eastern Europe. But there is no assurance this is the case — just a possibility. The only way to be certain is to continue our interrogation of Orion. Would you agree?"

The Prime Minister did not immediately reply. She sat at her desk looking out the window to the American Embassy across the expanse of Parliament Hill. Brad knew better than to interrupt her thoughts. He waited quietly. In a moment, she turned to look at him.

"Yes. I agree, Mr. Randall. Continue with your interrogation. But I am not very happy with the direction in which all this appears to be taking us. As a government, we may be left vulnerable — a position I can ill afford at this time."

Brad made no reply. He waited. She looked at him.

"I know. That is not a matter for you. Very well. Go ahead, but keep me informed, particularly if it should transpire that some senior official in External Affairs becomes suspect."

She walked to the green baize door as she spoke and opened it for him.

"Do try to bring me some good news some time," she said as she ushered him out.

The interrogation teams did not have the luxury of time in which to spin out their questions. Brad and George McCain discussed the problem with Marcel Lepreau and Patricia Haley. She expressed it succinctly.

"Normally, we would have continued to question him about Gadenus while at the same time pursuing the leads he has so far given us about a possible spy in External. He's shrewd. Our lack of questions about Gadenus will have made him realize that we have been successful in that quarter. Unfortunate, because, if he is a 'wrong un', that could be very helpful to him."

Patricia Haley shrugged, as George McCain spoke quickly.

"Don't worry. It's not your fault. To keep knowledge of our success concealed from him would have taken a couple of additional days. We simply can't afford that amount of time. Keep at him. The last bit he gave you about a code-name — Cue-tip — is interesting but doesn't get us very far. His other comment that he remembers being told that Cue-tip was the object of an unsuccessful recruitment attempt in the '60s could be the break we have been looking for. We've started the search of the records. The problem is that the approach may have gone unreported, as so often is the case. We simply wouldn't know about it. If that idiot in Parliament — the one who keeps hollering about too much secrecy and the need to make all these cases public to inform the taxpayer — had his way, we wouldn't have *any* such cases reported.

"It took the better part of the day to get that much out of him. He's a difficult, unpleasant character. I keep telling myself that it's the sheer ugliness of the man, but it is more than that. There is something about him I can't stand. Like finger nails drawn across a blackboard."

"Well, you may not like him Patricia but he seems to like you and it shows in your team's interrogation results. Close your eyes and keep at it."

"I wish I could close my eyes. I don't know which is worse — with his contacts or without. The colour of his eyes changes but not the expression."

John Merrivale pushed his chair back and stared at the papers piled on his desk. He removed his glasses and slowly began to clean them with a piece of soft lint he kept in his desk drawer. The records search had turned up 182 recruitment attempts which were known to have been made against government employees by the KGB and their friends in the preceding ten years. God knows how many other such attempts had gone unreported, perhaps including the attempt to compromise Cue-tip.

He rubbed his eyes and replaced his glasses. He picked up the sheets of paper on which he had been writing in his copperplate hand, and examined them carefully. Of the reported cases, 91 were employees of External Affairs. A little more than half were male. There was nothing in Orion's testimony which indicated Cue-tip's sex but Merrivale accepted McCain's hunch that the suspect would turn out to be male. The majority of the female employees were in the secretarial or clerical grades. Merrivale set aside the list of these until he had examined the files on all the male cases involved, 43 in all.

The statistics derived from the records search were compiled on a world-wide basis. They included attempts which had been against government employees in places as distant from one another as Singapore, Havana, Pretoria, Buenos Aires and Moscow. Merrivale decided to examine first those against whom recruitment attempts had taken place in Soviet bloc countries, including Cuba. There were 18. He eliminated from these all those males who by the beginning of the decade were not in a Foreign Service Officer class or equivalent.

He was left with a list of nine names on a single sheet of paper. Sorting through the piles of files set on a large table at the end of the room, he extracted the relevant ones and began a painstaking, minute examination of each one. It took John Merrivale several hours more work since many of the files were incomplete. He had to ask for material cross-referenced to other files — three of which were in the special counter-espionage files. In other cases he had to seek the information he wanted directly from the Personnel files of the Department of External Affairs. The result was a short list of three names: Charles de Cabourg, Edward Terence York and Hugh

Barrington Portland. All of them were presently senior officers. All of them had been the object of a recruitment attempt. Two of them, York and Portland, had reported the attempts, which apparently were unsuccessful. In de Cabourg's case the attempt had only become known through a defector who came into British hands. De Cabourg's failure to report the attempt to blackmail him probably adversely affected his prospects for a couple of years, but there was no evidence to suggest the attempt to recruit him had been any more successful than in the case of the other two. All three of them were likely candidates to be "Cue-tip".

De Cabourg although still on the strength of External Affairs was presently on loan to the National Defence College. Terence York was abroad, having been appointed eighteen months earlier as Canadian Ambassador to the Republic of Ireland. Hugh Portland was a Deputy Under Secretary of State for External Affairs and rumoured to replace the present Deputy Minister, a French Canadian who was said to be anxious to move and was in line to head Canada's delegation to the United Nations in New York.

Merrivale extracted the paper on which he had written the particulars of Portland's personal history and career. It was an impressive record. It also made Portland potentially a most attractive target for recruitment by the KGB. Merrivale knew Portland, having served with him on one or two of the committees in the intelligence community which also dealt with security questions. He liked the man. He was intelligent and personable. It was difficult to believe he might be a Soviet agent. Yet, if experience was any guide, it was precisely such persons in the past who had fallen prey to KGB blandishments. Perhaps Portland's claim that the attempt was unsuccessful was a deliberate lie. From the report, it had amounted to one rather crude attempt to compromise him with a KGB "swallow" in a Leningrad hotel. Perhaps there had been more to it than Portland had reported. Maybe they had tried to compromise him on some other ground — something that Portland would not want to have his employer know — homosexuality, perhaps, although there was nothing on record to suggest such a proclivity. It was a rule of thumb in the Security Service that where human nature was involved nothing was impossible. If Portland had been successfully compromised on some such ground, then his reporting of an attempt against him could have been a clever move to disguise the fact — something the KGB could well have authored.

John Merrivale examined the sheet of foolscap on which he had summarized Portland's history. There was nothing in it which aroused the least suspicion, except the attempt to compromise him when he was posted to the Canadian Embassy in Moscow. His marriage was unsuccessful but there was nothing about the sad mess which suggested KGB involvement. He read through his incomplete handwritten notes.

Hugh Barrington Portland.
Born, June 12th, 1931, Upper Musquodoboit, Nova Scotia.
Father; Edward Linsey Portland.
Mother; Emma Gooch Krause.
Elder brother died of pneumonia, 1929. No other children.
Barrington family of United Empire Loyalist background, immigrating to Nova Scotia, 1783.
Primary school near Upper Musquodoboit.
Family moved to Halifax, 1945.
High School, Halifax.
Dalhousie, B.A., 1952.
McGill, M.A., 1954.
Successful Rhodes Scholar, 1954. Did not take up scholarship.
Entered Department of External Affairs, FSO 1, 1955.
Minister's Office, 1956.
Canadian Delegation to the U.N., 1958.
Early 1959 married Juanita Cassimira de Ramera: (Born, Sept. 8th, 1936, Aguadilla, Puerto Rico. Father, Luis Alegria de Ramera. Owner of clothing factory and active in local political life.) Member of U.N. Secretariat 1958-9.
Late 1959, a daughter born.
Divorced, 1961. Mother given custody of the child.
Starts Russian language training.
1961, posted as Second Secretary, Canadian Embassy, Moscow.
Late 1963, unsuccessful attempt by KGB to compromise him (see Special file K.5930A-P).
1964, returned to duty in Ottawa.

From 1964 to the present he had advanced steadily, filling increasingly responsible jobs at home and abroad. It was a good career and from the rating reports given him over the years, it also was a very successful one. There was no doubt he was well qualified to take over the top job in External Affairs. By the same token, if he were a KGB agent he could hardly be better placed from the Russian standpoint — a valuable asset which the KGB would go to some lengths to protect.

After the Prime Minister was informed of the latest results of Orion's interrogation she instructed a small select committee to be struck, chaired by the Secretary to the Cabinet, to examine the matter. She was particularly upset that Hugh Portland stood high on the list of suspects. He had become one of her favourites — someone to whom she turned increasingly for advice on foreign affairs, and whom it was evident to those in the know that she looked forward to appointing as Deputy Minister.

"I can't believe that Hugh Portland is anything but a loyal Canadian. Surely you don't think he could be a spy?"

She turned angrily to Brad.

"Like you, Prime Minister, I find it very hard to believe. But there have been occasions in the past when the most unlikely people have turned out to be spies — public servants, journalists, politicians, lawyers, university professors and businessmen — the KGB have catholic tastes."

"But what does this do to the operation of the government? How can I trust anybody?"

Brad returned her angry stare.

"Normally, we would attempt to resolve the doubt by direct confrontation after we had collected sufficient information to make this possible. In this case we have too little upon which to act. We could, however, confront him if you wished."

"No. I don't want Hugh Portland confronted. Such a course of action would be traumatic for him, especially if, as I believe, there is absolutely nothing to support the suspicion. In the circumstances the doubt probably could not be resolved and the effect upon him would be devastating. The only humane course is to continue your investigations and for the select committee to evaluate the evidence. I want the minimum number of persons privy to the suspicions about Portland and the others on the list. I don't like it. I don't like it one little bit."

Brad cleared his throat.

"If our investigations are no more conclusive than they have been, we may want your authority to extend them."

"What do you mean?"

"Surveillance. Perhaps even the use of intrusive methods."

"No. I won't hear of it. These people are quite innocent. We have nothing but the word of this man . . . ."

"Orion?"

"Yes. Nothing but his evidence. It isn't even evidence. Just a hint. I will not have Portland harmed on such flimsy material. Is that clear?"

"Yes. However, Prime Minister, the information Orion provided us with about Gadenus turned out to be accurate — all too accurate. There is no doubt that Gadenus has done a great deal of damage. In the circumstances, we have to believe that Orion's information about a spy in External also is genuine."

The Prime Minister rose from her chair and walked to the window. After a moment she turned. Wearily, she spoke.

"Very well. But go carefully — and don't touch Portland in a way that might harm him without my specific authorization. Keep me informed."

Brad knew from experience the interview was finished. He withdrew. He sympathized with the Prime Minister. None of them liked the climate of suspicion created by Orion's revelations. If it had not been for their success with Gadenus and the accuracy of the information provided to the Americans, Orion's information could be dismissed as mere disinformation. The Russian defector's lead about "Cue-tip" had to be taken seriously. He wished there was some means of speeding up the inquiry — some shortcut they could take. Brad sighed. He had been in the business long enough to know there were seldom any shortcuts — nothing in counter-espionage went smoothly or quickly.

As if to prove Brad's point, the next two days went badly. Orion fell ill with some virulent form of intestinal disorder. The doctor prescribed antibiotics which cured the disease, but it was three days before interrogation could resume. His illness left Orion irritable and unco-operative. At noon on the fifth day Brad received a call from George McCain on the intercom.

"Can I see you?"

"Urgent?"

"Yes."

"Okay. Join me in the 'cubby-hole'."

Brad could tell little from George McCain's expression as he took the seat opposite him.

"Good news?"

"Depends on how you look at it. Orion said something this morning which could be important in pinning down the identity of 'Cue-tip'."

"What did he say?"

"Marcel and Patricia were taking him round the course for about the twentieth time — you know — could he be more specific about when he first heard about 'Cue-tip'? Could he not remember who had told him? As you know, he has been vague about these and other points. In the course of his replies, most of which were not very helpful, he made the comment that he was told that 'Cue-tip' spoke Russian. They were careful not to react, but as soon as the interrogation ended they ran the tapes through the latter part of the morning's discussion. There is no question about it. He said that 'Cue-tip' speaks Russian. I thought you would want to know as soon as possible."

Brad let out a slow whistle.

"What does this do to our list of suspects?"

"I haven't had time to look at it but it is my recollection that

Hugh Portland speaks Russian. Perhaps there are others on the list as well who speak the language."

"Get John Merrivale and his boys on this right away. They will have to examine the entire list — male and female suspects."

George McCain and Brad met John Merrivale at 6:15 p.m. in the "cubby-hole".

"Sorry to have taken so long, but when we began examining the list of names from the standpoint of which ones knew Russian we ran into problems. The data provided by External on language training and proficiency proved to be inaccurate or simply lacking. For example, one of the first names we looked at was a Jacqueline Albert, who had served twice at the Embassy in Moscow in a reasonably senior clerical grade. There was nothing on her file to indicate knowledge of Russian, yet it was obvious that in two tours there, even if she didn't use the language in her work, which she didn't, she would have acquired some knowledge. Happily she is now in Ottawa and we were able to confirm that she has a pretty fair command of the spoken language."

John Merrivale paused briefly to take some papers from his briefcase.

"Although I am not confident we have all the data, it seems there are eleven persons on the list who have proficiency in Russian. Two of them, who are of Russian or Ukrainian extraction, speak the language fluently. In the case of one of them, Russian was her first language. Like the others on the list, they both have been the object of attention by the KGB. Of the remaining nine, Hugh Portland is the most senior and, it so happens, the most fluent. It appears that he has a flair for learning languages. In my opinion this particular test places Hugh Portland at the top of the list of suspects. He is by far the most obvious candidate to be 'Cue-tip'."

Brad Randall's worst fears about the Prime Minister's reaction to this latest development were confirmed when he saw her in the company of the Secretary to the Cabinet. In anticipation of her reaction he had persuaded the Secretary to the Cabinet to accompany him, on the grounds that he had a duty to do so in the light of his chairmanship of the select committee. At least it meant that he didn't take the full brunt of her anger and frustration alone.

"I suppose you now are going to ask me to approve surveillance of Hugh Portland?"

The Prime Minister glared at Brad.

"Yes, Prime Minister. This latest information certainly leads us to the inevitable conclusion that Portland is the most likely suspect. The only way we have of testing those suspicions, apart from direct confrontation, is to place him under surveillance."

"What do you mean by 'surveillance', Mr. Randall?"

"I mean everything. Complete surveillance."

"Bugging his telephone?"

"If it is going to be effective, Prime Minister, it will have to be more than merely interception of his telephone calls."

"Why? Why do you have to go to such lengths?"

Brad made an effort to hide his irritation. She knew the answer full well. God knows she had approved similar intrusive methods in the past.

"If Portland is a Soviet agent, he has to communicate. Without some means of communication he is useless to them. We would wish to intercept his mail, and his telephone and telegraph communications. We probably also will wish to install electronic surveillance in his apartment and to search it."

"Search it? You mean surreptitiously?"

"Yes, Prime Minister."

"Why? What possible use can that be?"

Brad sighed, avoiding the quizzical look which the Secretary to the Cabinet cast in his direction.

"Because, if he is a spy he may have the means of communicating with his masters in Moscow concealed in his apartment. With the tremendous advances in electronics in recent years, the KGB have developed some very impressive and sophisticated communications gear, so small that it can easily be concealed in the covers of a book. Only a search will tell us if Portland has such equipment or any of the other paraphernalia of the spy — one-time cypher pads, micro-dot equipment, large sums of cash or false documentation."

The Secretary to the Cabinet spoke slowly.

"I'm afraid that Mr. Randall is right, Prime Minister. He has taken us about as far as he can with the present investigations. To resolve the doubt, one way or the other, we need more information about Hugh Portland than we possess."

The Prime Minister stared at the Secretary to the Cabinet without speaking.

"There is one further point I should make, Prime Minister. I think the time has come to tell Hugh Portland's Minister. Until this point I believe you have felt that the matter should not be made known to your colleagues. I think that was the correct stance so long as Portland was only one among several whom we suspected might be a spy. Now with the evidence pointing strongly in Portland's direction and, if he is to be placed under intensive surveillance, I think his Minister should be informed. Among other things his Minister will wish to be guarded, without being obvious, in his dealings with Portland henceforth."

The three of them sat in silence while the Prime Minister played with a silver letter opener. The metal caught the reflections of the lighted chandelier overhead. Brad was reminded of a film he had seen as a child in which an evil sorcerer mesmerized a beautiful young girl by letting a silver pocket watch hanging from a heavy silver chain turn before the girl's frightened eyes.

"Very well. You may go ahead with your surveillance. But don't expect me to like it."

The Secretary to the Cabinet spoke.

"Do you wish to speak to the External Affairs Minister or would you prefer that I do so?"

"I would prefer that you do it. Make it clear that only the minimum number of persons are aware and that I want it kept that way."

Brad intervened.

"Prime Minister, I suggest the senior official in External responsible for security and intelligence also should be made aware."

"Why?"

"Because as the investigation progresses, we may want a contact in External other than the Minister. In addition, if the British are to be made aware — a proposal I was going to place before you — then I think the Senior External official responsible for dealing with them also must be made aware."

The Prime Minister looked angry.

"Why should we tell the British? It's none of their damned business."

Brad hesitated momentarily, but knew that he had to press on.

"In the normal course of events I would agree. However, we know that Hugh Portland is due to fly to England next week on business. We do not have the means to keep him under surveillance outside Canada. We will have to ask our British friends to help. Even if we did have the means, we would be chary of making the attempt — among other things it would be a direct contravention of our long-standing agreements with them. We could try to engineer some excuse for cancelling the trip but in the circumstances that would be difficult without arousing curiosity among Portland's peers and, more important, with Portland himself. If he is what we suspect, that would be a mistake."

The Prime Minister did not immediately comment. She continued to toy with the silver letter opener. Finally, she placed it on the desk.

"Very well. I agree. You have made your point. You may tell the British. I hope you make clear to them that the information should be closely guarded. If Hugh Portland is clean, he had better emerge from this unscathed. I don't want him turned into damaged goods if he has done nothing wrong. Is that understood?"

"Yes, Prime Minister. I will make the point strongly to the British. They have not let us down on that score in recent years.

Since we are seeking their help in this matter, we can do no more than trust in their discretion and professionalism."

Eight

"Jesus. Nothing. Absolutely nothing. We've been over that apartment with a fine tooth comb, twice. Nothing. Physical surveillance produced nothing out of the ordinary. Electronic surveillance, interception of his telephone and mail have drawn a blank — a large duck's egg. He has to be clean. The only excitement was the trip he made to the Soviet Embassy — some bloody diplomatic reception — the kind of thing his job requires him to do. We managed to have someone near him the whole time — someone as fluent as he is in Russian. Nothing. All the Russians spoke to him about was disarmament and wheat. Hardly the stuff of which espionage is made."

George McCain slammed his hand on the table in the "cubbyhole" where he, Brad and John Merrivale were gathered.

"It certainly looks as if he's clean. I'm a bit reluctant to make that official until we have a few more days behind us. Are you sure he hasn't been using some dead letter drop?"

George McCain replied.

"Absolutely sure. The surveillance boys haven't let him out of their sight for a moment. Hell, they even followed him to the urinal in the Chateau Laurier. For the most part, he leads a pretty quiet life. He has a girl-friend, but even his love-making is unexciting and predictable. She's a widow. We've checked her out ten different ways. Husband was an Air Canada pilot with an RCAF background. Nothing the least bit suspicious."

John Merrivale intervened.

"I think George is right. We've been over the surveillance reports in great detail. The results suggest nothing the least bit suspicious. I even did yet another review of Portland's de-briefing after he reported the incident to his Ambassador in Moscow. The Ambassador made his report to External, using the diplomatic pouch for the purpose. That is to say, the Ambassador decided not to use the embassy's telegraphic cypher facilities — at the time there was some suspicion that the Russians were reading our cypher traffic. Some time later one of our people flew to Moscow to de-brief Portland. There was a further de-briefing when he returned to Ottawa, early in 1964."

Merrivale reached for a glass of water on the table before him.

He drank slowly, his Adam's apple working as he did.

"The attempt to compromise him was unexceptional, even rather crude. In fact it had a certain air of hasty improvisation about it suggesting that some eager member of the Leningrad KGB was trying to make a name for himself. According to Portland, and the Embassy records bore him out, he was asked at the last minute to substitute for the Ambassador at some diplomatic function organized by the Russians. In the circumstances, the Foreign Office gave the necessary approval — normally it takes several days to get permission to travel outside Moscow. Portland was there two nights in an hotel arranged for him by the Soviet authorities. When he returned to his hotel room after an official dinner on the second night he discovered a most beautiful, black-haired woman in his bed, stark naked. According to Portland, he recognized it was a set up and immediately left the room and raised hell with the old crone who was the "housekeeper" on his floor. Since this didn't achieve anything, he claims he went to the manager on the ground floor and made quite a fuss. This achieved results — by the time he returned with the manager to his room the girl had disappeared. There is no way of corroborating his story but there is nothing about it which suggests he was lying. The Embassy sent a note to the Foreign Ministry complaining about a member of the mission being importuned in this way. The diplomatic note, which was numbered, was merely acknowledged — nothing more."

Brad sighed.

"As you can imagine, I am under some pressure from the Minister for External Affairs and others. They don't like the situation — they want results. I can't say I blame them. Let's give it until the beginning of next week. If the situation is the same, I'll have to let them know that we have been unable to discover anything to confirm the suspicions about him. The obvious next step would be confrontation, but I rather doubt the Prime Minister will agree. It will be her decision. I'm sure she'll resolve the doubt in his favour without confrontation."

Two days later Brad's secretary, Rosemary, called him on the intercom.

"Matt Villier's calling you from Washington on the secure line. The red 'phone."

Brad picked up the telephone receiver.

"Matt."

A woman's voice answered.

"I'll put Mr. Villiers on now."

"Brad? Matt here. I thought we'd better use this line. Silas asked me to call you."

"Trouble?"

"Yes. But first, Silas has instructed me to brief you on Firefly.

He still doesn't know that I've already done so. I'm now authorized to tell you everything I've already told you."

"Thank you."

"You'll make whatever notes you must so that your records will demonstrate that you found out today?"

"Will do. Now what's the trouble?"

Brad waited.

"He's dead."

"Firefly?"

"Yes. He died last night from an apparent overdose of heroin. As you know, they have had to keep him on it, hoping gradually to wean him off."

"I'm sorry to hear it."

There was a pause at the other end.

"There is more, I'm afraid."

"What?"

"They did an immediate autopsy. The pathologists are divided in their opinions about the actual cause of death. One school believes that his general physical condition was so poor that even a minimal overdose could have killed him. The dosages were strictly prescribed. There is some evidence that the amounts in his blood stream were considerably higher than they should have been. They do not think death was accidental."

"You mean they think he was murdered?"

"It's a possibility. The difficulty is that we probably will never be able to know for certain."

"Where the hell does that leave us?"

"Well, if he was murdered, only the KGB stood to gain. Needless to say we have started a full-scale inquiry. It will take time. Silas thought you should know since this might have some bearing on your investigation of Orion."

"If 'Firefly' was murdered by the KGB it certainly will. Damn! Nothing in this business is simple."

Matt chuckled.

"Don't tell me you're only finding that out now — thirty years later?"

"To hell with you, Villiers. Please thank Silas for me. This needs to be thought out carefully for reasons you well know."

Matt's guarded reply came back.

"Yes, Brad, most carefully."

"Okay, Matt. My love to Louise."

Brad asked McCain and Merrivale to join him in the "cubby-hole". He gave them the gist of his conversation with Matt Villiers.

"What's your opinion? Does this change our view of Orion?"

John Merrivale replied.

"If we were certain that 'Firefly' was murdered by the KGB, it might. If they did murder him, why? What was the motive? It's not readily apparent to me. However, simply because we can't think of a motive doesn't mean they didn't murder him. But if they did murder him, why wait until now?"

George McCain grunted.

"As far as I'm concerned it doesn't change matters much one way or the other. I can see that, in certain circumstances, 'Firefly's' murder could be interpreted as casting doubt on Orion's credibility. But the information Matt gave you is too uncertain for that. I say we're no further ahead. Just another puzzle — as if we didn't have enough already."

Brad stood up and removed his jacket.

"Hot in here. The damned air conditioning hasn't been work-ing for the past week. I guess you're right — the information about 'Firefly' doesn't change much. We'll simply have to keep it in mind as we progress. I think the interrogation teams should be told as soon as possible. It certainly doesn't change anything as far as our coverage of Portland is concerned. Okay, let's get on with it."

Two days later as Brad was preparing himself to inform the select committee that they had drawn a blank on their surveillance of Portland, he received a telephone call from Halifax, from Paul Gribanov. As he picked up the 'phone, Brad glanced instinctively at the clocks at the end of the room. 1326 Ottawa time. 1426 in Halifax. He wondered what Paul was calling about.

"Paul. How nice to hear your voice. What's up?"

From the stutter at the other end of the line, he knew Paul was excited.

"Brad. Yes. Patricia."

The line appeared to go dead.

"Paul. Are you there?"

"Yes. Patricia. She's had a boy. Eight pounds, one ounce."

He was so excited that it was difficult to follow him.

"Patricia's had the baby? A boy? Congratulations. How is she?"

"Yes. A boy. Eight pounds, one ounce."

"Great, Paul. But is Patricia okay?"

"Yes. Patricia's fine. The boy is well."

"When did this happen?"

"Sorry?"

"When was the baby born?"

"This afternoon. Two hours ago. In hospital. I'm still at the hospital."

"That's the best news I've heard in a long time. Congratula-tions. Have you decided upon a name?"

"Sorry?"

"Have you a name for the baby?"

"No. We can't decide. I want Nicholas. Patricia wants Patrick."

"Both good names. Why not Patrick Nicholas?"

"Perhaps."

"How are things apart from being a father?"

"Good. Business is good. I'm taking courses at the university — at Dalhousie."

"Good. What kind of courses?"

"Classics. In the classics department. Latin and Greek."

"Good. That's a great idea, Paul."

"Oh, that reminds me, Brad. You remember the egg?"

"The Fabergé egg?"

"Yes, the one my mother sent."

"What about it?"

"I remember something she told me about it — years ago. I was reminded by one of the courses I am taking."

Brad fought to supress the excitement he felt.

"What did you remember?"

"I think she said that the Fabergé egg was given to my great-grandfather or my great-great-grandfather. I can't recall exactly. I think it was my great-grandfather. Anyway, he received the egg as a present from some nobleman for having rescued his son from drowning. Later they had a fight over the egg and the nobleman shot my ancestor. He died from the wounds he received but, before doing so, he is supposed to have uttered the latin phrase from Virgil's Aeneid; "Timeo Danos et dona ferentes". I remembered the story while reading the Aeneid."

"Isn't that the bit about, "Beware of Greeks bearing gifts", or something like that?"

"I think a more precise English translation might be, "I fear the Greeks even when offering gifts'."

Brad expelled his breath noisily.

"Same meaning for my purposes. Paul, are you sure about the story?"

"No. I'm not sure. There was more I think, but I simply can't remember. If it hadn't been for studying Virgil, I probably wouldn't have remembered anything. Is it important?"

"Yes, Paul. It is important. You cannot possibly imagine how important. When did you remember?"

"Oh, a couple of days ago when I was working for a paper I have to prepare for my professor. Patricia hasn't been sleeping and I forgot about it. I had to call the doctor since I thought she had started her labour. It turned out to be a false alarm."

"Paul, I cannot thank you enough for this information. Some day I may be able to explain its significance to you. In the meantime, congratulations to you both and much love to Patricia."

With his mind probing the various possibilities opened up by

Paul's information, he reached for the intercom.

"Rosemary. Patricia Gribanov has had a baby boy. Could you have the protective detail in Halifax arrange to send her a large bunch of roses with a note from me. They will know how to go about it. It will be a personal charge. When you find out how much it is, I'll make out a cheque to whoever pays for it. Could you ask McCain and Merrivale to join me as soon as convenient?"

Neither George McCain nor John Merrivale reacted strongly to Brad's account of his conversation with Paul Gribanov. John Merrivale spoke slowly.

"Taken together with the fact that our intensive surveillance of Portland has produced not a shred of evidence to suggest he is a KGB agent, it certainly looks as if Orion's a plant. It's a pity we didn't learn the secret of the Fabergé egg sooner."

McCain snorted.

"I've never been happy about the bastard from the beginning."

Brad looked from one to the other.

"I take it you agree that I let the select committee know of this development immediately and that we recommend that Portland be given a clean bill of health?"

Both men nodded their assent.

"Very well. I will arrange to do that as soon as possible. In the meantime, George, will you make sure the interrogation teams are fully briefed. They will want to change their tactics and perhaps even the strategy — I leave that to you to work it out with them. I doubt that we will be able to trip him up — he's too wily for that but we may get lucky. Clearly the weak spot in his testimony is what he has told us about 'Cue-tip', but when you look carefully at it he hasn't told us much. He never identified Portland — he let us do that for ourselves. He's clever and slippery. The teams will have their work cut out. Tell them to go back to work on 'Stallion' with him, as if we hadn't solved that one yet. That should throw him. I will try to get agreement to tell our American and British friends that we think he is a plant and why."

The select committee were unanimous in agreeing that Portland should be considered "clean" and that the surveillance of him should be lifted immediately. The Secretary to the Cabinet drew Brad aside after the meeting.

"The PM should be told at once. Unfortunately, I have a commitment to fly to Winnipeg with the Minister of Justice. In fact I'm supposed to be on my way to the Department of Transport hangar now. Can you arrange to see her as soon as possible? Tell her of the select committee's view about Portland. She will be pleased. No doubt she will wish to inform the Minister for External Affairs herself."

"Okay. Will do. I'll also ask her if she has any objections to my telling the Americans and the British — we certainly owe them that one."

Brad was unable to see the Prime Minister until the afternoon, following question period in the House of Commons.

"Mr. Randall. I hope you have good news?"

"Yes, Prime Minister. For once I do have good news."

She listened attentively to what Brad had to tell her, including his proposal that the Americans and the British be informed, to which she offered no objection.

"I am relieved. I never thought for a moment that Hugh Portland could be disloyal. What are you going to do with this man . . . ?"

"Orion?"

"Yes, Orion."

"I'm afraid that we will have to continue our interrogation of him. If he is, indeed, a plant, as Galena Nadya's message suggests, we would like to get him to confess and to learn the full extent of his mission. To achieve this may not be easy. He is obviously a skilled professional."

"I don't like it, Mr. Randall. If this man's presence here becomes public knowledge, it will cause a lot of questions — questions by the Opposition, questions from the press. The government's position is not strong. I don't like it."

Brad remained silent. Ever since Paul Gribanov's electrifying information about the warning Galena Nadya clearly intended to convey, he had been turning over in his mind a scheme. Maybe it would work, maybe it wouldn't. If it failed, nothing would be lost — if it succeeded, it would solve the problem bothering the Prime Minister. He hesitated a moment before plunging ahead.

"Prime Minister, I have a possible solution. Would you agree that I try to arrange a meeting in Europe with Galena Nadya Gribanov?"

"You mean in Russia?"

"No. That would be too risky and, from my standpoint, impossible. I had in mind somewhere in Western Europe. I am due to attend a regular meeting at NATO headquarters in the near future. I would try to arrange to have my NATO meeting coincide with a meeting with Galena Nadya. It would attract less attention than making the trip specially for that purpose. It might not work. It would be risky for her, and I haven't much time in which to arrange it. I could ask my Amerian friends to get a suitable message to her. They have the means if they are prepared to help. I will have to act at once."

"What would you hope to achieve by such a meeting?"

"At the very least to obtain details of Orion's mission which would enable us to crack his cover story. However, if she is able to meet me I would hope that also would mean she is prepared to re-defect."

"You mean to return to Canada? Why would she do that?"

"The fact that she sent the message suggests she may already have such a move in mind. She may already have prepared the ground for her departure. That she has revealed to us that Orion is a plant can only mean she is prepared to work against her masters — the KGB. When she learns that she has a grandson, I suspect she will have a very strong personal motive to defect again."

"Grandson?"

"Yes. I ommitted to mention that the real purpose of Paul Gribanov's telephone call was to tell me that Patricia, his wife, had a son. I would, of course, include that information in whatever message I send her."

The Prime Minister stared at Brad across her desk. To Brad's relief a slow smile spread across her face.

"Mr. Randall. I had not quite appreciated until now what a devious mind you have. I suppose you have discussed your plan with your colleagues?"

Brad smiled back.

"No, Prime Minister. I have kept my own counsel on this one. For one thing, I wasn't sure I was going to make the proposal to you. Anyway, it seemed wiser to keep it to myself. If you agree that I might make the attempt I do not intend to tell anyone else, except, of course, the CIA. In a matter as risky as this, experience tells me that the fewer people involved the better."

The Prime Minister picked up her silver letter opener and balanced it on the tips of the fingers of her left hand. Suddenly she pulled her hand away and let it fall to the desk.

"Very well, Mr. Randall. You have my agreement to what you propose."

Recognizing the signs that the interview was ended, Brad started towards the door.

"Oh, Mr. Randall . . . "

Brad turned. The Prime Minister was smiling.

"You will be careful, won't you?"

"Yes, Prime Minister. I will be careful."

It took Rosemary a couple of hours to track down Matt Villiers in Washington and to arrange for the secure line to be hooked up.

"Matt. There has been an important development. We have good reason to think that Orion is a plant. We wanted you to know this immediately. If we are right in our belief, it will have as much importance for you as it has for us. Firefly and Stallion may be only throwaways. The other suspicions he has broadcast would appear to be a disinformation ploy. Will you inform Silas for me? I would have called him direct but there is another matter on which I need your help."

"Okay, thanks. I'll get the information to Silas. Now what do you want from me? What's the problem?"

"I need to get a message to someone in Moscow."

"Someone in Moscow?"

"Yes. You remember Galena Nadya Gribanov?"

"You want us to deliver a message to her? That's a pretty tall order."

"I know, but it's very important. For all of us."

"She's a Colonel in the KGB. Am I right?"

"Yes."

"I think we can arrange it, but I have to have Silas's okay. It's one for DDP. How soon?"

"Well, that's the problem. Like yesterday."

"We couldn't guarantee anything, and probably couldn't even confirm the message has been delivered."

"I understand. Will you do it?"

"In principle, I don't see why not. There are risks but they should be acceptable. What's the message?"

"You better write it down."

"Okay."

"It reads — 'Grandson. Quadri's Café Venice. Noon 8, 9, 10 October.'"

"I'll read it back."

"Good."

"Let's leave it, Brad, that if you don't hear from me further tonight the deal is on. Again, I can offer no assurances."

"I understand, Matt. Many thanks again for your help. Oh, Matt. One final point. I would be grateful if you and Silas and anyone else handling the message deal only with me. Okay?"

"Understood, Brad."

As Brad replaced the telephone receiver he wondered if he had done the right thing. The risks were enormous. The message might never be delivered. It might reach her and result in her arrest and execution. He sighed. Only time would tell.

Nine

As Brad appreciatively sipped the large martini-on-the-rocks which the Sabena stewardess served him, he began to relax. The last few weeks had been difficult — running something as unusual as a security service was always demanding. That he recently had also been acting as a glorified "case officer" merely served to increase the pressures. He was grateful to J.B., his predecessor and mentor, for having successfully persuaded skeptical Treasury Board officials that the head of the service should travel first class on transatlantic flights. Since such trips were an increasing necessity, often on short notice, the privilege was particularly welcome. He knew from experience the strain associated with attending NATO security and intelligence meetings in Brussels almost immediately following a seven-hour flight. At least this way, he might get a few hours sleep, something he knew was virtually impossible in the crowded, noisy conditions of economy class. The high-pitched scream of some infant in the rear section reminded him of what he was escaping.

The more important part of his mission could be even more demanding — in intellectual and emotional terms. The latter consideration he was reluctant to admit, even to himself. If Galena Nadya showed up in Venice . . . If she had received the message he sent her through CIA channels . . . If she understood it . . . There were so many "ifs" — so many risks and unknowns in what he was about to do.

Was his choice of Venice as a rendezvous wise? Would it have been safer and easier for Galena Nadya to meet him in Helsinki, Berlin or Vienna? Perhaps, although he rationalized that Venice was about the same distance from Moscow as those places. Too late to worry now. The die was cast. He had to admit his choice of Venice, in part at least, was based upon nostalgia. He and Gwenneth, in the early months of their marriage — before it turned sour — spent a marvellous six days there. Shortly after their posting to Germany they managed Easter in Venice. It was a particularly happy time for both of them — perhaps the happiest time of their few years together. He wondered if Galena Nadya knew Venice. He tried to remember details of her interrogation. He could not recall her ever saying that during her early years with her father she had visited Italy. It seemed unlikely her more recent KGB service in Moscow would have taken her to Venice. Somehow he hoped not. He wanted to be the first to introduce her to its marvels and delights.

During the second day of the NATO committee's discussion, his Italian opposite member, Giuseppe Casardi, turned up. Brad approached the Italian at the mid-morning coffee break.

"Giuseppe. I was afraid you had decided to skip the meeting."

"Brad, my friend. How nice to see you again. I remember with pleasure your kindness last year at the special committee on terrorism in Ottawa. How is Marianne?"

"She is well, thank you. Busy as usual, but well. I have a favour to ask."

"Anything, Brad. Anything. I have not forgotten your help in providing us with information about the links between the XXII anarchist groups and Henri Curiel in Paris. It was crucial to the case. With the help of the French it led us directly to the Feltrinelli's group in Milan. What can I do to repay you?"

Brad put his coffee cup on a table beside him.

"Well, Giuseppe. I plan a few days in Venice, immediately after these meetings — a holiday. I know Venice only slightly. Can you recommend a small hotel? Not too expensive. Nothing as grand as the Amigo, where I am staying here, but the same ambiance. Not some large American-style hotel. As a precaution and to avoid attracting attention I will use another name. Connors, my middle name, will serve."

"When will you be there?"

"As soon as these meetings are finished. I understand we are likely to finish before noon tomorrow. If possible I would like to be in Venice tomorrow night. I would be there the 8th, 9th and 10th."

"Are those dates important?"

"Important only in the sense that they are the only time I can afford."

"I understand. Will you be alone, my friend?"

Casardi smiled as he asked the question. Brad laughed.

"No, no, Giuseppe. Nothing like that. A single bed will be fine. You Italians!"

Casardi shrugged his shoulders.

"Sorry, Brad, but these matters are important. Let me think about it for a bit."

"Fine. I was going to suggest that if you are free tonight we might dine together — you would be my guest, I hope?"

"Delighted, Brad, delighted."

"Good. You know l'Epaule du Mouton, off the Grande Place? How about eight o'clock, if that's not too early?"

"Eight o'clock it is. I admire your choice of restaurant. By then

I will have a few suggestions about Venice. A holiday, you say?"

"Yes. I need a few days rest. It has been a hectic Fall."

Brad was certain from the expression on his face that Casardi didn't believe him. He had not expected that he would.

L'Epaule du Mouton was located on a short, narrow street running off the Grand Place in Brussels. It was a favourite of the Brussels cognoscenti — Brad had been first introduced to it by the Head of the Belgain service, General de Gentilhomme. Not large — it could seat no more than twenty — its wine-coloured velvet upholstered banquettes along each wall, the mahogany woodwork, and crisp white linen tablecloths had a turn of the century air to them. He could imagine Edward VII or, for that matter, his grandson Edward VIII, being ushered through the frosted and bevelled glass doors. Brad arrived at the restaurant a few minutes before eight. The owner and Henri, the ancient servitor, flanked by faceless, silent acolytes in their teens, greeted him warmly.

"Bonsoir, Monsieur. Mais oui — notre soufflé au chocolat est toujours au menu, mais il faut le commander à l'avance. On en reparlera plus tard, si vous voulez."

Brad made a point of having at least one meal in the establishment whenever he visited Brussels which, in recent years, was a frequent occurrence. He liked the place — the quiet atmosphere, the serious, solicitous, leisurely approach to the enjoyment of superb wines and delicious food. Giuseppe Casardi arrived as he and the white-aproned waiter were discussing the menu du jour. The owner and the waiter greeted Casardi warmly. Agreement was quickly reached on the choice of aperitif.

"At the risk of appearing disloyal to the aperitifs of my own country, I suggest the Spanish fino — a real fino from Sanlucar de Barrameda. I recommend it."

They settled down to the important first business of deciding what to eat and drink. Upon Henri's advice, for their main course, they both settled for the suprême of pheasant Berchoux — breasts from a pheasant hung for four days, with a stuffing made of black truffles, pheasant liver, cognac, and lemon juice. The meat was napped with a Saint Florentin sauce and garnished with crusts of puff pastry filled with cooked pheasant leg meat and minced mushrooms. To accompany this dish, Henri recommended a bottle of 1969 grand vin de Beaune-Grèves, vigne de l'enfant jesus. To accompany the quenelles de brochet with sauce Nantua which Casardi chose and Brad's crayfish in dill, at Casardi's suggestion, they had a bottle of Soave Classico — a delightful plain, dry, straw-coloured wine.

"It has to be drunk young, even after three years it loses its freshness."

They decided to accept Henri's recommendation of cheese for

dessert rather than the sweet chocolate soufflé which Brad hankered after.

"I think you would find the soufflé a bit too rich following the pheasant, Monsieur. The pheasant dish needs a sharp foil — a pont l'eveque or a ripe camembert. It would go well with the Beaune."

Henri re-filled their glasses with the fino.

"I have thought about your holiday in Venice. I have a few suggestions. I even took the liberty of making some preliminary arrangements — if you do not like them they can be easily changed."

Casardi sipped the sherry appreciatively.

"The easiest and the most interesting way to get there from here is to fly to Milan and to take the train from there to Venice. The 'rapido' is clean and comfortable — especially in first class, which I recommend. If the weather is half decent the view of the lakes and the alps is spectacular."

"Sounds fine to me, Giuseppe."

"There is a plane from Brussels which will get you to Milan and allow you to catch the 'rapido' about three o'clock. I have made a reservation in the name of Connors. You can pick up your ticket at the airport. I will have your train tickets tomorrow and a reservation in first class. Once you get to Venice, I would suggest that Aldo Crespi meet you at the railway station. He is a Venetian. You have met him I believe?"

"Yes, I have met Crespi. But there is no need for you to go to so much trouble, Giuseppe. It is only a holiday."

"My friend, even if it is only a holiday, it will help to have someone who can speak the language, who knows the city and who could offer help if it is needed."

"Giuseppe, Giuseppe. You have been too long in the business. It's a holiday, nothing more."

"I may have been too long in the business, but when the head of a service such as yours takes a holiday in Venice there has to be a reason. It's none of my business. So long as you are in my territory, I feel a responsibility to make you welcome and to see that nothing goes wrong. Aldo Crespi will meet you at the railway station. He will be available while you are in Italy."

"Thanks, Giuseppe. I accept the offer gratefully."

"Good, that's settled. For an hotel I suggest a small place just off St. Mark's square — the Antico Panada. It is comfortable, the restaurant is small but excellent. You won't find many North American tourists there. The owner happens to be a friend of ours. I have taken the liberty of telephoning him. He has reserved the best room for you."

Brad laughed.

"You certainly don't do things by halves."

Casardi smiled. He spread his hands, palms up.

Some mechanical failure delayed the departure of Brad's flight from Brussels to Milan, resulting in a wild and expensive forty-five kilometre taxi ride from Milan's Malpensa airport to the Central railway station, where he caught his train with only minutes to spare.

As the train picked up speed, Brad began to relax and took stock of his surroundings in the comfortably clean first class compartment in which Aldo Crespi had reserved a seat for him. Fighting his way through the crowds on the platform with the effective aid of an agressive, mustachioed porter of indeterminate age and a vast vocabulary of Italian expletives, brought home to Brad the wisdom of the arrangements which Crespi insisted on making. Without a reservation he probably would have stood the whole way to Venice; the second class carriages resembled giant sardine tins.

There were only two other occupants of his compartment. A middle-aged woman whose aristocratic features, well-cut suit, brown alligator purse and monogrammed cigarette lighter suggested money — generations of money. The second occupant, a young man of slim build, swarthy features, a mass of carefully-barbered curly, black hair, wearing a dark grey flannel suit, black leather gloves and a very expensive pair of hand-made black leather loafers, had the appearance of an executive of some multinational bank or corporation. Neither of them invited intercourse. Indeed, they studiously avoided it. The woman immersed herself in a paperback book, the Italian title of which Brad was unable to decypher. The man busied himself with a mass of papers he took from a black leather briefcase, fitted with expensive gold combination locks. Brad looked out the rain-streaked window at the passing landscape — a not very inspiring vista of kilometre after kilometre of farmland, vineyards and ugly, cement block buildings of different shapes and sizes. His mind turned again to Galena and their meeting.

Perhaps the attempt to meet her was a mistake? Perhaps he was reading too much into the message he believed she intended to convey? "Timeo Danaos et dona ferentes", the famous line from Virgil's Aeneid — I fear the Greeks even when offering gifts — could only have one meaning in the context it was used. Perhaps the invitation he sent her through CIA channels involved too great risks for her to accept? Perhaps she never received the message? The questions without answers went round and round in his head.

At least if something did go wrong it could not be blamed on a leak from the Canadian end. Only the Prime Minister knew and approved of what he intended to do and she was unaware of any details. Normally he would have informed his colleagues about his plan to meet Galena. Some instinct prompted him to keep his plans to himself. Brad acknowledged that subconsciously he was suppressing a desire to examine his motives for carrying out his plans in such secrecy — he did not like to admit that he entertained doubt about the security of his own organization. His last minute approach to Casardi would remain unknown in Ottawa since he contrived to attend the NATO meeting without bringing along an assistant as he sometimes did. The help he obtained from the CIA should also be secure. It was channeled directly through Matt Villiers, whose discretion he trusted completely. Matt understood the request was personal and not for dissemination.

As the train drew to a brief halt in Brescia, the rain stopped and sunshine broke through the clouds. By the time the train began to skirt the southern end of Lake Garda, the cloud cover completely dissipated, providing a breathtaking view of the lake framed by the mountains beyond. For the remainder of the journey Brad was totally absorbed in watching the changing landscape between Verona and Padua against the dramatic backdrop of the gradually receding Alps.

As they drew near Venice, after crossing the Brenta River, the terrain became flat and marshy, criss-crossed with narrow canals and irrigation ditches, between which were strips of lush, thick vegetation. Brad knew something of the history of the *campagna*, the Venetian hinterland where, in the sixteenth, seventeenth and eighteenth centuries, wealthy Venetians built sumptuous country villas on *terra firma*, surrounded by rich fields and small vineyards. Brad regretted he did not have time to approach *La Serenissima* by gondola across the lagoon separating the city from the mainland. In its heyday the area along the river must have been a bucolic playground for Venetian noblemen and their families. In those days a good gondolier could make the journey to St. Mark's square in under two and one half hours and a letter sent in the morning very often was answered by nightfall.

Brad's reverie, which had turned to unpleasant thoughts about the efficiency of modern postal services, was interrupted as the train slid to a halt in the Venice railroad station and the noises of debouching humans welled up from the platform, through the lowered carriage windows. With a formal, barely perceptible bow on the part of his two travelling companions which he imitated, he left the compartment ahead of them to join the swelling mass of noisy passengers making their way towards the station steps leading to the Grand Canal.

He could see no sign of Aldo Crespi. Hefting his suitcase, he made his way slowly down the wide stone steps. He thought he might take one of the *Vaporetti*, the steam launches which act as water buses throughout the city. It might give him a chance to see something of the city. However, discouraged by the long lines of jostling, shouting Venetians attempting to make their way home on the overcrowded boats, he turned to a nearby sign advertising "taxis". He was accosted, in English, by the driver of a powerful looking, noisy motor launch.

"Taxi, Mister? You want taxi?"

Brad didn't like the look of the driver. Unshaven, albino features, wide-spaced stained teeth, long white unkempt hair under a ridiculous leather cowboy hat; he did not inspire confidence. However, at the moment there were no other choices.

"St. Mark's square. I want to go to St. Mark's square."

He had to shout to make himself heard among the surrounding noise.

"Okay. I take you."

"How much?"

The man shouted something which Brad could not hear.

"How much?"

For reply the man held up both hands, spreading the fingers. He did this twice and held up the fingers of his right hand once. While Brad was trying to make the calculation — twenty-five thousand lire in Canadian dollars — the man grabbed his suitcase and started to stow it in the cabin of the boat, which was bobbing wildly in the waves created by a passing *vaporetto*.

"Hey, wait a minute. I . . . "

Before he could finish the sentence, he felt a hand on his shoulder.

"Mr. Connors. I'm sorry I missed you in the station. An unfortunate mix-up. A thousand apologies."

Brad recognized Aldo Crespi's voice.

"Aldo. I'm certainly glad to see you. I was trying to get to my hotel. This character snatched my bag before I could make up my mind."

Crespi, who was dressed in an olive brown raincoat, a brown jacket, grey flannel trousers and an open sports shirt, looked quickly at the water taxi and the driver. He smiled.

"That's fine, Brad. I suggest we go with this taxi."

To Brad's annoyance, they sat in the stern of the boat while for the next few minutes the driver tried to drum up other customers. Finally, Brad remonstrated with the driver who responded with a tirade in voluble Italian which, although Brad couldn't understand, he sensed was not complimentary. After a second encounter, the driver grudgingly shoved off. As they made their way through the narrow waterways, Aldo tried above the noise of the engine and the exhaust, to point out various points of interest. Where the taxi rejoined the Grand Canal the driver pulled up to a nearby barge anchored to act as a loading and unloading platform for passengers. He shouted to two very good looking Alitalia airline stewardesses waiting on the dock. After a quick verbal exchange they jumped down into the taxi.

They docked at St. Mark's square and the stewardesses disembarked without, as far as Brad could see, any money changing hands. Brad picked up his suitcase and extracted twenty-five thousand lire from his wallet. He offered it to the driver and was greeted by a tirade in Italian.

"Fifty thousand."

"You bastard. You said twenty-five."

The taxi driver made as if to block Brad's path and reached for his suitcase. Aldo Crespi, who had said nothing to that point, put his hand on Brad's shoulder.

"You go ahead, Mr. Connors. I wish to attend to this."

Stepping around Brad, he spoke quietly and rapidly to the driver, who looked surprised and frightened. Crespi took a small identification card set in heavy plastic from an inside pocket and showed it to the man. Brad would have said that in the absence of any colouring in the man's skin it would have been impossible for him to pale further, but he did. His cheeks took on a putty grey hue and his pink eyes looked as if they might bulge out of their sockets. He started to say something in a cracked voice. Crespi cut him short with a chopping motion of his right hand.

"Alright, Mr. Connors. I suggest we go."

Brad still had the twenty-five thousand lire in his hand.

"I suggest you put those in your wallet, Mr. Connors."

"But . . . "

"The driver is glad to have conveyed you. He has indicated he regards it an honour to have been able to have been of service to you. I told him you were a guest of the State — a distinguished American. As you can see, he understands completely."

The look on the man's face was one of abject terror. Brad almost felt sorry for him. As they walked away from the mooring, Brad turned to Crespi.

"My God, Aldo. I don't know what you did, but you sure scared the hell out of him."

"He was lucky I didn't order his arrest and he knows it. He operates without a licence from the municipality, although the law cannot prevent him from taking passengers. He is a pirate and a crook, preying on tourists. I told him I had a note of his name, which appeared on the motor launch's papers tacked to the bulkhead, and that I would request the Caribinieri to place him on their watch list. He knows that could mean that his boat may be confiscated. I think it will be some time before he tries his little extortion tricks again."

As they crossed St. Mark's square the light took on the luminous quality peculiar to sunrise and sunset in Venice in spring and autumn. The mosaics on the Church of San Marco and the grey stone of the ducal palace were bathed in a shining, yellow light. The new red bricks of the re-built Campanile — the clock tower — took on a soft hue they never possessed at other times of the day and season. They stopped amid a large flock of pigeon attracted by a young girl with an enormous sack of corn, which she broadcast liberally.

"Beautiful."

"Yes, Mr. Connors. One of the most beautiful sights in the world."

While they spoke, the quality of the light changed again. Darkness did not fall at once although to Brad it seemed as if it had. For the first time, he noticed lights in some of the buildings surrounding the square. The bell in the clock tower boomed out the hour. In response, as if on cue, scores of pigeons rose, beating the air with their outstretched wings. Banking in perfect formation, they flew twice around the square before settling in another quadrant to continue their shameless soliciting of tourist bounty.

"The Antico Panada is just across the square, to the left of San Marco church. I'll lead the way."

After registering into the hotel, he stood Aldo Crespi a couple of drinks before they parted company. Brad appreciated the manner Crespi went about the chore given him by Casardi.

"Should you require anything — anything — you have but to request it. You can call either of these telephone numbers at any hour of night or day."

He handed Brad a piece of paper on which the numbers were neatly typed. Brad placed the paper in his wallet.

"Thanks, Aldo. I don't imagine I will need help, but thanks all the same. I just plan to sightsee and to enjoy myself."

Aldo Crespi smiled.

"We understand, Mr. Connors. However, should there be anything — anything — please don't hesitate to ask. We are here to make sure your 'holiday' is successful."

"I am most appreciative. You already have been extremely helpful"

They shook hands.

Brad went to bed early after an excellent dinner in the small restaurant of the hotel and a walk around St. Mark's. Under a full moon, the square and the narrow streets leading into it were filled with strollers. The cafés were crowded, including Quadri's where he hoped to meet Galena. The different orchestras vied with one another for the attention of the crowds. Brad wondered if Galena was already in Venice. Perhaps she also was in the square? He had no doubt that Aldo Crespi and his friends were following his movements. He shrugged. In the circumstances, perhaps it was not such a bad thing. If Galena was able to escape to Venice and keep their rendezvous, there was no assurance that she might not have been followed. In that event, Crespi's help might be very welcome.

He awakened to the sound of the bells in St. Mark's square. From the bed he could see blue sky through a crack in the heavy wooden shutters. Before going to bed, with difficulty, he had managed to pry open the hermetically-sealed windows. Italians, it seemed, feared the night air.

As Brad shoved the shutters open, the sound of the bells reverberated off the walls of the room which were brilliantly lit by the sunlight. Perhaps the fine weather was a good omen for his meeting with Galena. He hoped so.

Ten

Brad took breakfast in the room where he had dined the night before. In daylight the room seemed much larger. By the time he finished, it was nearly ten o'clock and he had the room to himself. Still two hours before noon, the time selected for his rendezvous with Galena. He admitted to being nervous. Perhaps he was on a wild goose chase. To fill in the time he decided to exchange some of his travellers cheques for lire. He made enquiries of the concierge, a tall, distinguished man with the demeanor of a foreign minister rather than a hotel factotum.

"The American Express office? Yes, Mr. Connors. It is not far from the hotel. I will show you on the map."

Spreading a tourist map of Venice on the counter, he marked the location with a ball-point pen.

"We are here, on the Calle Larga San Marco. You walk to San Marco Church, across the Piazza San Marco. Take the arcade by the Museo Correr and continue along that street. The American Express office is on the right-hand side. You will see the sign over the door."

Brad thanked him and was about to walk away when the concierge interrupted him.

"Your passport, Mr. Connors. We have finished with it."

Brad took the document and put it carefully in his wallet. He could never get used to the European practice of requiring passports when registering in hotels. He assumed it was mainly for police purposes. There were times when he wished they had something similar in Canada. Damn it, in Canada passports were not even required for the millions of visitors who crossed the border from the United States each year. There were no exit controls — there was no way the Canadian authorities could know if a person entering the country, subsequently left it. He could imagine the Italians, the Germans or the British operating such a system!

Completing his currency transactions, he still had three-quarters of an hour to wait. He decided to walk back to St. Mark's square and along the Grand Canal on the Riva degli Schiavoni. He was not alone. The streets were filled. Although the sun was strong, a brisk wind from the Adriatic lowered the temperature of the air. Brad was glad of his raincoat. Waves, driven by the wind, splashed against the stone embankment, throwing up occasional spray. To his unpractised eye the water seemed perilously close to the top of the embankment, no doubt as a result of the tide and the phase of the moon. Passersby seemed not to notice him or the water level. Brad walked back the way he had come, not daring to turn off into the maze of side alleys and bridges behind the Doge's Palace for fear of becoming hopelessly lost.

He went to Quadri's early and took a table in the corner from which he could survey the whole scene. He glanced around to see if he could spot Aldo Crespi on his tail. There was no sign of surveillance. By twelve-thirty the tables around him began to fill with tourists and Venetians enjoying the early spring sunshine and the good weather. No sign of Galena. He read the *Herald Tribune* and ordered a negroni. He found the mixture of gin, campari and soda particularly suited to Italy. At one o'clock he ordered a Genoa salami sandwich and coffee. The salami was excellent, but the bun surrounding it had a tough crust which scraped the roof of his mouth. There was no one remotely resembling Galena in the café. All his earlier doubts returned. He cursed silently.

By one-thirty the tables around him began to empty. By two o'clock there were only a handful of customers in the restaurant, the remainder presumably having gone home to a siesta. Soon the only others left were an obviously German couple with a bag of camera equipment which would have done credit to a CBC cameraman, a couple of teen-age girls who might have been of any nationality, an American with "Cornell University" spread across the back of his faded blue windbreaker, which fitted well with his neat grey beard, crumpled pork-pie cloth hat and blue jeans, and an elderly woman reading *Paris Match*. No Galena. Brad decided to give it another fifteen minutes. Nearly three hours of fruitless waiting made him edgy. Damn. He would have to repeat the process the next day and the day after. As he was about to leave, the American, wearing sunglasses with mirrors for lenses, brushed past his chair.

"Inspector Randall. Follow me. Hotel Flora."

Startled, Brad turned. The speaker could only have been the American who now was walking slowly in the same direction Brad had taken in the morning to reach the American Express. Brad followed. He found it difficult to believe his quarry was Galena. Although the words had been spoken softly, there was no mistaking what had been said. He stayed about fifty yards behind, having no difficulty keeping the "Cornell University" windbreaker in sight. At the Lisbona Hotel, after crossing a bridge, the trail continued along the Calle Larga 22 Marzo. The street became crowded and Brad narrowed the gap between them. As they reached the Saturnia International Hotel, the blue windbreaker turned sharp left down a narrow street. He followed quickly in time to see the figure disappear into a building with the sign "Flora" over the door. Entering the hotel, he saw the American standing by a door leading to a garden at the rear of the hotel. Brad followed into the garden which was deserted but for them. They went to a table in the far corner of the garden.

"Galena?"

Brad found it difficult to ask the question.

"Yes, Brad. It's me. I apologize for the beard, but I had to do it."

She removed the sunglasses. Brad stared at her. The eyes were Galena's. Although more deeply set in their sockets, they had lost nothing of their mocking quality. Her hair, dyed black and closely-cropped, altered her appearancc. She looked tired and pale, her skin was drawn tightly across her cheek bones. There were shadows under her eyes. Her lips were without colour but still as well-shaped and sensous as he remembered — and still turned upward ready to smile. The beard beneath was an obscenity.

Time also had changed him, but not as much as she had feared. The lines about his mouth and on his forehead were more pronounced, but that merely accentuated the features she remembered and liked. His eyes still had a sparkle and when he smiled, the laugh lines at the corners seemed deeper. His black hair, now flecked with grey, was almost white around the temples. The hair on his forehead had hardly receded at all. He was a handsome man. Obviously he had kept himself in good physical shape. His stomach was flat. No ugly paunch which seemed so much a feature of many men in middle age. His hands were unchanged; strong fingers, immaculate finger nails, a hint of nicotine stains. In so many ways he reminded her of Anatoli Ivanovich.

They sat looking at one another, saying nothing. Suddenly they both started to speak at once.

"Brad, I . . . "

"Galena, thank God . . . "

They laughed. Their hands reached out and touched. Hers were cold.

"Are you alright? Your hands are like ice."

She withdrew them quickly.

"It's nothing. I haven't had much sleep lately. I suppose I must be tired."

Brad was surprised. It was the first time he had ever heard Galena Nadya admit to any weakness.

"Brad, how is Paul? Is it true that I am a grandmother? Is the baby well? Is Patricia alright?"

Her questions came tumbling out. Brad laughed.

"Easy, Galena. Yes. You are a grandmother. Paul is fine. Your grandson and his mother are very well. Here, I have some pictures."

Fishing in his wallet, he produced polaroid photographs; one of the baby alone, two others of the three together. Galena slowly examined them. Her eyes filled with tears.

"He's beautiful! Strong. Look at those features, like my father. And his hands — so well formed. He is big. How much does he weigh?"

Brad grinned.

"I have no idea, Galena."

"Why not? I thought you were head of the security service these days?"

He teased back.

"You forget. Unlike the KGB, we don't investigate small children. I think Paul said he was 7 or 8 pounds when he was born. But I may have that wrong."

Galena threw back her head and laughed. The beard gave her a Mephistophelean appearance.

"That bloody beard. Can't you get rid of it?"

Galena's eyes mocked him. She stroked the small beard with a slender hand.

"Why, Brad. I thought it might please you. I can get rid of it if you want. However, before I decide to do that perhaps we ought to discuss the future — assuming I have a future?"

Her appearance may have changed but not much else, Brad reflected. She had always managed to come quickly to the point.

"That depends upon you — what you intend. I assume you have no thought of returning to the Soviet Union?"

"You haven't lost your knack of asking the right questions, have you? No, Brad. I have no wish to commit suicide."

Brad grinned. He placed his hand on hers.

"Sorry. I didn't mean to needle you. If you wish to come back to Canada, it can be arranged. However, there are some things I need to know before that can be decided. For example, the defector we call 'Orion' — he claims he is really Igor Petr Molodny, Colonel in the KGB. It was only recently that the message you seemed to be conveying through the choice of the Fabergé egg finally dawned on us. I think you were telling us that Orion is not a defector. That he's a plant. Am I right?"

"Yes. You are right. Molodny was sent on a disinformation mission. A complicated mission intended to sow doubt and discord among some of the more important NATO countries. I knew nothing of the planned operation until after we received information that Paul was still alive. It was being run by Department A of the First Chief Directorate. I was co-opted when it was learned that Paul was alive and probably under the protection of the RCMP."

"How the hell did the KGB discover that Paul was alive? More important, who was the source?"

Galena smiled, but it was a worried smile.

"As far as I know, all they learned was that Paul survived the explosion and the sinking of the *Nefertiti* and that subsequently the RCMP gave him protection. They also learned that Paul was married to Patricia Ballantyne. It was not clear whether the protection being provided was a form of custody and arrest or protection from the KGB. I never learned the source."

"Needless to say, the fact that he was alive in Canada placed me in jeopardy. Many of my colleagues viewed me with suspicion. I have had to be careful, very careful. The Head of the First Chief Directorate was an old comrade of my father's — he never said anything, he didn't have to. For months now there have been signs that my work was being monitored. It hadn't quite reached the point where the Special Investigation department of the Second Chief Directorate was involved."

Brad remained silent, thinking through the implications of what she had said. He believed her when she said she did not know the source of the information about Paul's survival. More than a score of people in Canada had known about Paul's escape, although only a few knew of the key role he had played in Operation Scarab. Since that aspect seemed unknown to the KGB, their information could have been provided by a low-level Residentura source. God knows there were enough of them. It could have been a political leak. Cabinet ministers had been briefed. It could also have been from a source within the Security Service. That could not be ruled out. Nothing could be ruled out."

"Were you involved in 'Operation Orion', if I may call it that?"

"We call it 'Operation Cobweb'. Since it was decided to base the operation in Canada, Department A were looking for some way of establishing Orion's crdentials with the Canadian authorities. Several ideas were considered and discarded for one reason or another. After it was learned that Paul was alive, they conceived the plan of using me to provide Orion with some message, some proof that he was a KGB officer. I suggested he carry the Fabergé egg, with a message for Paul inside it, delivering it only to you. I explained that the egg was a family heirloom which Paul would know could only have come from me — the genuineness of the message could not be in doubt. What I omitted to tell them was the history of how the egg came into the Gribanov family. I hoped Paul would remember, although I told him the story many years ago, when we first returned to Russia."

"Why Canada?"

"What do you mean?"

"Why did the KGB decide to base the operation — Operation Cobweb — in Canada?"

Galena smiled.

"I don't know, but I can guess."

"What's your guess?"

"Nothing personal, Brad, but your service has been in such a state of disarray in recent years that it's a sitting duck. The First Chief Directorate probably figured the odds of succeeding with such a complicated disinformation scheme were better in Canada than in any other NATO country. You have to admit you have been having your share of problems?"

Brad grunted.

"Okay, Galena. I get the picture. Don't rub it in. When Orion gave me the Fabergé egg, he claimed he didn't know how it had come into his possession, that it had mysteriously appeared in his apartment in Moscow with a slip of paper attached to it on which were my name and the initials RCMP."

"Yes. I believe that was part of the cover plan involving his defection. What he said, of course, was untrue as is his claim that he is a genuine defector. The deception plan is complicated, involving a couple of 'throw-aways' in Canada, at least one in the United States and one in Britain."

"I hope we can go into those matters in detail, later — in Canada. That would be very helpful. Obviously you received my message about this rendezvous. Was it then that you planned your escape?"

"No. Almost immediately after I learned that Paul was alive in Canada I started to plan my escape. Even before my involvement in Operation Cobweb, I could see the writing on the wall. When months went by without any reaction to the Fabergé egg message, I thought I had failed. If I hadn't heard from you, I planned to leave anyway. The message for this rendezvous was arranged through the CIA?"

Brad nodded.

"I thought so. It was professionally done. A fisherman on the Volga embankment. Since my plans were well advanced, I had only to time them in order to meet the dates you suggested. It involved a trip to Hungary which was not difficult since I've been directly involved in operations there. That was ten days ago. It took me nearly a week to cover my tracks, change my identity and make good my escape via an up-river Danube barge. An escape route I learned about some time ago, from dissident sources. Information not on KGB files. I reckoned it was too risky to use any of the rabbit runs used by the KGB to get in and out of Western Europe — once I was missed they would watch them all. My escape was not exactly comfortable. A narrow space built into the steel superstructure of the wheel house. It cost a lot of American dollars, but it worked."

"Do you think you were followed?"

"No. If I had been, I wouldn't be here now. I don't think they would have let me get beyond the border. As you know, the Danube, before entering Austria, divides Czechoslovakia and Hungary for about 80 kilometres. If they had suspected I was on a barge they certainly would not have let me through the checkpoints at Bratislava."

"What travel documents did you use?"

"An American passport. The passport is genuine. The entries are all forged. I did them myself. As you know, I have the training."

Galena withdrew the document from the leather purse slung over her shoulder, handing it to Brad, with a touching gesture of pride. Brad leafed through the passport.

"Congratulations. Most convincing. I see there is no Austrian entry, and no entry for Italy."

"That's right. My entry to Austria was a bit unconventional. I entered Italy on another passport. I avoided Vienna since that is one place the KGB will certainly look for me. However, since I took the trouble to create a few false leads, I fancy they will be concentrating their attention in the Baltic area — particularly Sweden."

Brad turned the passport to the page showing the holder's photograph and particulars.

"Stephen Nottman, born 8 July 1927, Little Rock, Arkansas. Good likeness, with that damned beard. Exactly the year of your birth, although not the day or month. If I remember correctly your birthday falls on April 8th?"

"Your memory hasn't failed you."

"Did you intend to enter Canada on this passport as Stephen Nottman?"

"No. I have another passport, in the name of a Danish citizen, Inger Jutson. Here."

She handed it to him.

"As you will see, she was born in Viborg on November 11th, 1929. I entered Italy with that passport travelling on the train from Graz. You will note the stamps show I entered Austria through Bregenz a month ago and was admitted to Italy yesterday. How do you like my handiwork?"

"At least Inger Jutson looks more like Galena Nadya, although that short hair certainly changes your appearance."

"If you like Inger better than Stephen I shall kill him."

With a quick movement she turned her back to Brad, placed her hands to her face and before Brad realized what she was doing, she had removed the beard.

"My God, Galena. That must have hurt like hell?"

"No, Brad. Modern science has done marvels for the theatrical world. Itchy, but nothing more."

She gently massaged her chin. Brad put his hand out and touched her cheek. At that moment the door leading to the hotel opened and a young girl, obviously one of the hotel staff, appeared. She looked embarassed.

"Mi scusino."

Making a curtsy, she quickly closed the door.

"My God, it's nearly seven. You must be tired and hungry. I'm famished. Do you want to go upstairs to your room and freshen up and we can have dinner somewhere?"

"Dinner is a fine idea, Brad. I would like to get out of these blue jeans and this windbreaker. I bought some clothes in Austria. But this is not the hotel in which I am staying."

"Not your hotel? Where the hell are you staying?"

"Not far from here. In a place called La Fenice et des Artistes, on the campiello de la Fenice. It's close by."

"But why did you come here?"

"It's such a beautiful, quiet garden. And there is only one entrance — through the hotel."

"Have you been to Venice before?"

"No, but I studied the city after getting your message. You forget the KGB has a very good library. Maps of every city to almost any scale."

La Fenice et des Artistes proved to be a short walk from the Flora. Galena led the way with assurance.

"How did you know about this hotel? It seems larger than the Flora."

"Oh, I read about it. I think it is nearly twice as large. I like the atmosphere. Do you want to see my room? It has a balcony."

Brad hesitated.

"Thanks, but no. While you're changing I have a bit of 'phoning to do about getting us back to Canada. It may not be easy on short notice."

Galena looked at Brad. Her eyes mocked him.

"Very well, but I may not make the invitation again. I won't be long."

"Take your time. I'll probably be in the telephone booth when you come down."

Brad called the first of the two numbers which Aldo Crespi had given him. There was an answer on the second ring.

"Si?"

"Do you speak English? My name is Connors. I would like to speak to Mr. Crespi, Aldo Crespi."

"Ah, Mr. Connors. Yes. Can I be of service? Commandant Crespi said you might call."

"Can I speak to him?"

"I can give you a number where he can be reached — 233745."

Brad repeated the number.

"233745"

"That is correct, Mr. Connors."

Brad called the number. A woman answered.

"Signor Crespi, prego."

"Un momento, prego."

After a pause a man's voice answered.

"Crespi."

"Aldo? It is James Connors. Sorry to bother you so late in the day, but I would like some help."

"Ah, Mr. Connors. Is everything in order? No troubles I hope?"

Brad laughed.

"No, no trouble, Aldo. Just that I would like two seats on a flight to Montreal for the day after tomorrow. One for me and one in the name of Inger Jutson, travelling on a Danish passport."

"Do you mind going via New York or Miami? It might be easier since there are many more flights."

"I would prefer not to go through the United States. Any flight which would take us directly to Montreal from anywhere in Europe so long as there are good connecting flights from here. Needless to say, I'll reimburse you immediately and if it is necessary I'll take first class tickets."

"I will see what can be done and leave word at your hotel. Anything else?"

"Yes. Would it be possible to use the resources you are using on me to cover the woman — Inger Jutson?"

There was a short silence at the other end of the telephone, followed by a low chuckle.

"I hope they weren't as obvious as that, Mr. Connors?"

"Not the least bit obvious, Aldo. In fact I haven't been able to spot them. I simply made the assumption that they were there — You just confirmed my assumption. The woman needs the protection more than I do."

"It will be done, Mr. Connors. Where is she staying?"

"At La Fenice et des Artistes. I am 'phoning from there. One more favour. Can you recommend a good restaurant? Something like L'Epaule du Mouton in Brussels?"

There was a pause.

"Harry's Bar on Calle Valaresso is good if you're in a nostalgic mood — Americans in Europe — the 1920s. The scampi Carlena are excellent. However, if you wish something a bit more Italian in atmosphere, I suggest Antico Martini on Campo San Fantin. Quite near La Fenice. The cannelloni are superb and the filet of beef in the chef's manner can always be depended upon. The house wines, Malvasia and Cabernet, are reasonable and excellent. If that fails I suggest La Caravella on the Calle Larga 22 Marzo. A bit further away. The other possibility is Do Forni on the Calle dei Specchieri. They usually have good grilled fish. It is quite a walk from La Fenice, although not far from your hotel."

"Thanks, Aldo. Thank you very much. For everything."

"Buona caccia."

As he replaced the receiver he saw Galena walk down the stairs. The transformation was startling. For the faded, patched and dirty blue jeans, running shoes and Cornell University windbreaker, she had substituted a burgundy suit of some soft material, with a cream coloured blouse. A smart pair of high-heeled leather pumps matched the colour of the suit. Lipstick, colour on her high cheek bones and her short, black hair completed the picture. She was stunningly beautiful and he felt old longings stir in his groin. She laughed as she caught the expression on Brad's face.

"You approve?"

She did a slow pirouette in front of him.

"You're very beautiful, Cinderella."

"Do you like the suit? I didn't get it at the GUM stores in Moscow. I found it in Graz. The blouse too — it's Italian silk. Sinfully expensive. Paid for with counterfeit U.S. traveller's cheques — the KGB are experts in the art."

She put her arm through his and smiled again.

"You promised me dinner."

The night was balmy. The full moon cast eerie shadows as they walked through narrow streets and across open squares.

"How is your Italian?"

"Not nearly as good as my English or German, but serviceable. Why?"

"What does buona caccia mean?"

"Good hunting. Why?"

Brad grunted. One up for Aldo.

"Oh, nothing. Just a phrase I picked up."

The restaurant was crowded. The head waiter looked at him superciliously. Did they have reservations? Before Brad could reply Galena spoke to the maître d'hôtel in rapid Italian, turning on the full force of her personality. They were quickly ushered to a small table along the wall at the rear of the packed restaurant. Immediately, the dirty dishes were whisked away and a fresh linen table cloth was spread. The headwaiter brought a vase with fresh roses and bowed to Galena as he placed them before her.

"How the hell did you do that? What did you say?"

Galena smiled.

"You North Americans! I simply told him we had motored a great distance to spend an illicit holiday together in Venice. That we were tired and needed the kind of rejuvenation which only dinner at his world-renowned restaurant could possibly provide. He believed me."

Her eyes mocked him.

"Jesus. I wouldn't want to be playing against you."

"You did once. Remember?"

"How can I forget? And I lost, too. That's a story I want to hear but it will have to wait. We have more urgent things to discuss."

"Such as food?"

She picked up the menu.

* * * * * * * * * * * * * * * * * * *

"Would you like a liqueur?"

"No, Brad. I'm content with this delicious wine. I would like an espresso, however. A memorable dinner. How clever of you to have found this restaurant."

"If it hadn't been for your charm and gall we might never have got in."

They were interrupted by the headwaiter leaning over Brad's shoulder.

"Signor Connors?"

Brad was surprised to hear his name. He looked up.

Bowing slightly, the man handed him a white envelope. Brad opened it. Inside was a couple of typewritten lines. It was signed by Aldo Crespi. He read the message slowly.

"The bearer of this will show you to the rear entrance. There you will be met by one of my men. Follow him. You both may be in danger. Urgent."

Brad looked at Galena.

"Trouble, I'm afraid. Here."

He gave her Crespi's message to read. She read it without comment and rose from the table. The headwaiter drew back her chair and motioned them to follow.

"But I can't leave without paying the bill. Tell him I want the check."

Galena spoke rapidly to the man.

"The bill has been paid by your friends."

They were led through the kitchens and along a narrow winding passage. They came to a locked door which the headwaiter proceeded to open with a large brass key. Brad pressed a ten thousand lire note into his hand as they squeezed by him. Outside they were met by a small man in a dark blue raincoat. He motioned them to follow and set off at a brisk trot through a maze of narrow streets. Suddenly they came upon a canal. They followed as he jumped down onto a stone landing. A long, powerful-looking motor launch was moored alongside. Aldo Crespi greeted them from the stern of the boat.

"Mr. Connors, Signora. My apologies for disturbing what I hope was an excellent meal. If you will come aboard I will explain, but we must leave here immediately."

He helped them into the boat and spoke to the helmsman in the wheel-house. From the landing, the man who had led them to the boat pushed the hull with his feet. The powerful engine sprang to life as they pulled into the canal and gathered speed. In a few minutes they were in the Grand Canal heading, as far as Brad could tell, towards the island of Giudecca and the famous Hotel Cipriani. Crespi spoke to the helmsman and the speed was reduced. The noise of the powerful engines died to a low purr.

"There. We can talk. My apologies for spoiling your evening, but the situation called for prompt action. I hope you will agree when you hear what I have to say. When we shifted our coverage from you to the Signora as you requested, routine counter-surveillance measures showed that she was already being watched by others. Indeed, these others followed both of you from the moment you left the hotel to go to the Antico Martini. There were two of them — very professional. Happily we had them outnumbered. One we were able to identify almost immediately. The other man we are having difficulty with. The one we have identified is Ivan Pavlovich Yatsyan, a Second Secretary at the Soviet Embassy in Rome. KGB."

Galena drew in her breath.

"Yatsyan? Are you sure?"

"Yes, Signora. He is well known to us."

Brad heard Galena say something in Russian under her breath.

"Yatsyan is a member of Department V — assassination. How did they get on to me? I could have sworn I was clean once I got to Austria."

Aldo Crespi looked at Galena with curiosity before speaking again.

"In the circumstances, I thought it best to take immediate steps to protect you. Yatsyan has a bad reputation with us, although we have never been able to pin anything on him. You will find your belongings in the cabin in your suitcases. Not very beautifully packed, but I don't think we missed anything. The hotel bills have been settled."

"My God, Aldo. You don't waste much time. You also paid the

bill at the Antico Martini. I must reimburse you."

Crespi smiled.

"Later, if you wish, although since you are our guest I don't imagine I will have much difficulty with the account. I had seats booked for you on a flight from Milan to Paris and from Paris to Montreal for the day after tomorrow. In the circumstances, I decided to alter the arrangements. You are now on a flight leaving Milan at noon tomorrow for Zurich and from there on Swissair to Mirabel. Because we were in a bit of a hurry I'm afraid I had to put you in first class on the transatlantic portion of the journey."

Crespi paused and smiled at them.

"Tonight I have arranged for you to stay in a safe house on one of the islands. You should be comfortable there and I promise you won't be disturbed. Tomorrow, the launch will take you across the lagoon to the mainland near Fusina. A car will pick you up and drive you directly to Malpensa airport. In case our KGB friends should be snooping around I have arranged to have you both pre-boarded. I assume the Signora is still travelling as Inger Jutson and will not use the other passport which is packed with her belongings?"

Crespi's innocent smile caused Brad and Galena to laugh.

"Yes, I will be Inger Jutson."

"The Italian in me is pleased. I don't think I would like you with a beard, Signora."

"I'm most grateful to you, Aldo."

Crespi spread his hands and laughed.

"You are our guest."

They had passed the island of Giudecca and were heading for another, smaller island. In a few minutes the engine was cut and they eased into a wooden jetty. They were helped ashore and followed Aldo Crespi up a narrow path. The helmsman followed with their bags. The house at the end of the path was screened from the water by a stand of cypresses and high bushes. Brad guessed they might be oleander. Crespi ushered them through the door. They were in an airy hall, tiled in marble. A beautiful curved staircase rose to the floor above. The house was much larger than it appeared from the outside.

"Heavens, a palace, Aldo."

"Not a palace, Mr. Connors, but comfortable. The housekeeper is Signora Piselli. She will look after you. Some of my men will be nearby during the night. Come, Signora Piselli will show you to the bedrooms."

Introduced in this manner, the housekeeper, a neat, attractive woman in her fifties, nodded and smiled. They followed her and Aldo up the staircase.

The adjoining bedrooms were large with a connecting door. Each had a king-size bed and a private bathroom. Doorways opened on to a common balcony, overlooking the lagoon. The lights of Venice were in the distance.

"I asked that the blinds be left open. I seem to remember that North Americans and the English do not like our custom of drawing the blinds at night. I did not know the Signora's preferences."

Galena did not immediately respond. She went onto the balcony. The noise of a ship's bell drifted across the water. She turned to them.

"I too like the windows open, Mr. Crespi."

"If you feel like anything to drink or eat you have but to call Signora Piselli. The house phone is beside the bed in both bedrooms. She will serve you breakfast here about seven-thirty. You should be ready to leave the house about eight o'clock."

They said farewell to Aldo Crespi at the head of the staircase. Galena put her arm through Brad's arm.

"Which is it to be?"

"What do you mean?"

"Which bedroom do you want?"

"I don't care. They are both the same. Ladies should have first choice."

"In that case I'll have the one with the yellow curtains and bedspread. There is another option, of course."

Her eyes teased Brad as she smiled at him.

"I know, but neither of us would consider that very professional, would we?"

Galena turned to face Brad as they stood in the bedroom with the yellow curtains. She put her arms around his neck and drew him gently towards her. She smelled of a perfume he remembered — *Je reviens*. Her lips found his and he responded. Gently disengaging, she pushed herself away from him, her eyes serious.

"Thank you, Brad Randall. Thank you for so many things. You are right. It wouldn't be professional."

She leaned towards him and brushed her lips against his cheek before turning towards the bathroom. As she closed the door she said,

"It's such a pity we only meet professionally. Sleep well."

Brad closed the connecting door.

Eleven

It took a few seconds for Brad Randall to recognize his surroundings. He had fallen into a deep sleep following the enormous meal they had been served about an hour after leaving Zurich. The free champagne served in first class did not encourage wakefulness. He looked at Galena, asleep beside him in the seat by the window. In a foetal position, with the light brown rug drawn tightly about her, she looked like a child. Her features showed fatigue. The tensions associated with her escape and the unwelcome discovery that she was being followed by the KGB must have been tremendous.

Brad thought about what she had told him in the last twenty-four hours and particularly in the last few hours. Most of what she had revealed would have to be picked up again when she was formally interrogated, a requirement she accepted, albeit reluctantly.

"I know, Brad. There are many questions but I am prepared for them, although I'm tired — tired of the whole business."

It was the second time since their meeting in Venice that Brad had heard Galena admit to being tired. He wondered if she was ill. Certainly at times, she looked frail. The medical examination she would have to undergo prior to interrogation might provide a clue.

Her account of Orion's mission left no doubt the Canadian government had very nearly been victim of a carefully planned disinformation operation calculated to throw suspicion on senior officials and others. The willingness of the KGB to "blow" Gadenus and the realization of the extent of his espionage activities over the years in itself created disruption for the government. Galena's revelations about Orion's duplicity would be welcome news in Ottawa, and in the other capitals where he had spread his poison. The CIA, in particular, would be relieved to know their suspicions about one of their most senior members were unfounded.

Galena's account of the reason Igor Molodny accepted such a difficult assignment, involving as it did his permanent disfigurement, was at once horrifying and revealing.

"Since I had no direct involvement in Operation Cobweb, my information is second-hand at best. However, if the story I heard is true, I almost feel sorry for Molodny. I do not like the man. He is vain and always went out of his way to ingratiate himself with the KGB brass. Still, I have to feel sorry for him. He was coerced into the assignment through threats made against his seventeen-year-old daughter, Larissa. After Molodny's wife left him to run off with another man some years ago, he brought his daughter up alone. She is the apple of his eye. Recently, she had a part-time job in the KGB section assigned to the surveillance of foreigners. They went to Molodny and threatened to use her as a 'swallow' to 'entertain' third world diplomats and visitors — a prostitute. The threat was especially cruel since it was very well known that Molodny has a strong dislike of Asians and non-whites, particularly blacks — something you must have detected from his interrogation?"

"Yes. His bias is clear."

"The irony is that Larissa has already developed a taste for promiscuity, a fact she carefully concealed from her father. She would probably enjoy being a KGB 'swallow'."

Galena stirred in the seat behind him, turning to find a more comfortable position. He looked at her tenderly and recalled her recent comments about the names she had been given. When he had questioned her about them, she said

"Yes, Brad. Galena Nadya is a nice name. I like it. But it is not very Russian — at least it does not fit the ancient Russian practice of using a patronymic. One of my given names should have been derived from my father or a paternal ancestor. My mother, for some reason unknown to me, insisted I be called Galena Nadya. As you know, she died giving birth to me. My father felt strongly about honouring her last wishes despite the objections of his family. So, Galena Nadya I am."

Her account of the history of the Fabergé egg and how it came into the family was equally interesting and elaborated on the story Paul had told. A Gribanov ancestor worked as an estate manager for a large landowner, Count Vladimir Nicolai Spasskonya. The Count, who was thoroughly disliked by those who had the misfortune to live on his lands, was noted for his strength and his addiction to vodka. Galena's ancestor, however, earned the Count's gratitude by rescuing his small son from drowning in a swift-running river, risking his own life in the attempt. The impulsive Count Spasskonya rewarded his estate manager with the unusual gift of the Fabergé egg.

Subsequently, after a falling out between Spasskonya and Gribanov, Spasskonya, in a drunken rage, attempted to recover the Fabergé egg. In the ensuing struggle the Count fatally shot Gribanov. Legend has it that Gribanov, an educated man, on his deathbed uttered Virgil's, "Timeo Danaos et don ferentes". The murdered man's widow managed to take the Fabergé egg with her when she fled Spasskonya's estates with her children to make a new life in Moscow.

The overhead loudspeaker announced the 'plane would arrive in Montreal in thirty-five minutes. Galena uncurled and sat up. Lifting the shade, she peered out the window.

"I can see the ground. The trees have their new colours. My favourite season in Canada — the fall. It is good to be back."

Brad smiled.

"You certainly slept. Feel better?"

Galena opened her purse and examined herself in the mirror of the compact.

"Yes. However, repairs are in order. Excuse me."

When she returned, Brad marvelled at how rested and fresh she appeared.

"Montreal. My, that brings back memories."

"I imagine it does, Galena. Speaking of memories, I 'phoned George McCain from Zurich airport. He will meet us at the ramp. We'll drive directly to Ottawa and a safe house. I expect he'll have arranged for us to be excused the usual customs and immigration formalities."

"George McCain. How is he?"

"Older. As we all are, but well. Galena, I would like you to face Orion soon after we get to Ottawa. Are you up to it?"

Galena did not immediately reply. She looked out the window. He could not see her face.

"Yes, Brad. I am prepared to meet Igor Molodny."

The confrontation took place the second day after she and Brad returned to Ottawa, early in the morning. Brad was not present at the meeting between Orion and Galena but received an account of it from George McCain and Stanley Hydchuck.

"Her appearance completely took the wind out of him. He was flabbergasted to see her. The exchange between them was very unfriendly. Stan was able to follow some of it, but the Russian was too fast for him at times. Galena was spitting tacks. We have it all on tape but it will take time to transcribe and translate."

Stanley Hydchuck took up the narrative.

"As far as I was able to follow what was said, Galena accused Orion of having a subsidiary mission of finding her son's where-abouts and of setting him up for assassination. She went after him with the fury of a mother grizzly.

"Orion denied her accusation, saying she was paranoid. I thought she would hit him. His denials had the ring of truth about them, but she wasn't having any of it. She called him everything — her vocabulary is impressive. Words I've never heard but the meaning was clear. His continued denials increased her anger. She finally slipped the knife between his ribs when she mentioned his daughter,

Larissa. She called her a slut who would thoroughly enjoy being a KGB 'swallow'. I had the impression he wasn't completely surprised to hear what Galena said on that score. His reaction was pitiable. He almost literally collapsed. We were so concerned that we called for the doctor who put him on a mild sedative. He's a bit better now.

"On the central issue, of course, he has admitted he was a plant. He expressed willingness to talk, but it will take skilfull handling and a lot of time to sort out fact from fiction — genuine information from disinformation."

Brad had made an appointment to see the Prime Minister that afternoon. It was a meeting he would not soon forget. Determined not to be late again, he arrived at the Prime Minister's office fifteen minutes early. Although the House of Commons was adjourned, the office was busy, with a stream of visitors coming and going. He was kept waiting a half hour after the appointed time. The reason for the delay emerged, a Senator who had a cabinet portfolio. From the Senator's demeanor and his curt nod in Brad's direction, his meeting could not have been a success. When he was ushered in Brad recognized the symptoms — the Prime Minister was in one of the foul moods for which she was famous. He cursed his luck.

"'Well, Mr. Randall. You asked to see me. I assume it's about your captive spy again. What's his name?"

"Igor Molodny, Prime Minister. Also known as 'Orion'."

"Well, what about this Orion? What more have you found out about him? Have you now concluded that he was telling the truth after all when he suggested the Deputy Under Secretary of State for External Affairs is a spy? His information about the other man appears to have been accurate enough."

He felt like telling her to give him a call when she was able to be civil. Instead, he pushed ahead with what he had come to tell her.

"You will recall you authorized me to try to arrange to meet the KGB Colonel who sent us the message implying that Orion was not to be trusted. The woman, who several years ago acted as a spy for the Russians while on the Privy Council Office staff, is Galena Nadya Gribanov. After we unmasked her she agreed to work with us and then subsequently gave us the slip and returned to Russia with her son. You recall?"

The Prime Minister tapped her fingers on the desk impatiently.

"Yes, Mr. Randall, I remember all that. Get to the point."

"I managed to meet her in Venice a few days ago."

She raised her eyebrows.

"Venice, you say? A nice place to visit."

He could not ignore the dripping sarcasm.

"Yes, it is. It also provided a convenient and safe rendezvous. As a matter of fact, our Italian friends were so hospitable they prevented a KGB assassination of Colonel Grivanov. They probably, in the process, also saved my life."

The Prime Minister's hands were still.

"Go on."

"Galena Gribanov confirmed the meaning of the message we received from her. Orion was despatched to Canada on a disinformation mission designed to sow doubt and distrust within the Canadian government and among certain of our allies."

"Why did the Russians decide to mount such an operation here? Why not in the United States or Britain?"

Brad hesitated.

"Galena Gribanov did not know the answer to that question when I put it to her. She offered an opinion, however."

"And what was that opinion?"

"That because Canada has been unable to get its security act together in recent years, we presented opportunities for the successful launching of the operation — the Russians evidently call it Operation Cobweb — which do not exist in other countries of the alliance."

"Do you subscribe to that theory?"

The Prime Minister's voice took on a sharp edge which Brad had heard on other occasions in the past. Brad shrugged.

"It has some logic to it. As you know, in various ways we have been and we are vulnerable."

The Prime Minister rose from her chair and walked to the windows overlooking Wellington Street.

"Go on."

"After they discovered that the KGB had traced her to Venice and very likely were planning to assassinate her, our Italian friends were very helpful in arranging our safe passage out of the country. Galena Gribanov confronted Orion this morning. He admitted his real reasons for being in Canada and has agreed to co-operate with us. It will, of course, take time to unravel the tangled skein — to sort out the truth from the disinformation. It is quite clear, however, that our suspicions concerning the Deputy Undersecretary of State for External Affairs are without foundation. He was one of the intended targets of Orion's mission."

"I suppose we can be thankful for that."

The Prime Minister returned from the window and sat down. She placed her elbows on the desk and placed her fingers together in a pious gesture. Those who knew her recognized the gesture had little to do with piety.

"You like this woman — this Galena Gribanov — don't you?"

The question caught Brad off balance. He took time to phrase his response.

"Yes, Prime Minister. I do like her. I admire her strength of character. She is a patriot in the best sense of the word. She is courageous and she is intelligent."

"Is this paragon also beautiful?"

Although her words had a sharp edge, she uttered them with a smile.

"Yes, Prime Minister. I find her attractive. I suppose I always have."

"Thank you for your frankness. If you had said anything else I would not have believed you. I assume you would like to see her given asylum?"

"As you will recall, that was an integral part of my suggestion when I asked you to authorize my making contact with her. It is the price of her co-operation. I have told her that she may remain in Canada if she wishes. Since she has her son and grandson here under RCMP protection, it is not surprising that she wants to stay."

The Prime Minister said nothing. Brad waited.

"Agreed. What about this man Orion? How do you propose to get rid of him?"

Brad wished to God that he had not caught her in such a bitchy mood. What the hell was she getting at?

"I'm not sure I follow, Prime Minister. I wasn't proposing to get rid of Orion. There is still a great deal of useful information to be extracted from him."

"Useful to whom?"

"To the RCMP Security Service, to the government and to our allies."

"I don't give a tinker's damn about his usefulness to the RCMP or to our allies. He certainly isn't of any use to the government — only a potential embarrassment."

Brad's heart sank. Christ, that was it. Politics! He played for time, pretending to miss the point.

"I don't understand, Prime Minister. I assumed that the government would want to know everything it is possible to know about Orion's mission, if for no other reason than to be certain that there are no loose strings — unknown situations, like the attempt to throw suspicion on the Deputy Undersecretary of State for External Affairs, which could come back to haunt us in future."

The Prime Minister fixed him with an icy stare.

"That is a risk we will have to take, but it isn't anything like the risk we would run if Orion's activities became public knowledge. The sooner he is out of the country the better. If he remains here and his story becomes known, there probably will be a hue and cry for a trial. In political terms that would be very unwelcome at present. There are two by-elections coming up. As you know, my party lost in the last three by-elections. I can't — we can't afford another loss."

Damn the bloody woman.

"We haven't asked the opinion of Justice on the likelihood of obtaining a conviction if he were to be charged under the Official Secrets Act. On the basis of previous experience, however, I imagine the opinion would be that the chances of a successful prosectuion are slim."

"Exactly, Mr. Randall. In those circumstances the government would be accused of being soft on Communism. Our opponents would be able to hammer us at a very awkward time. I want him out."

"But, Prime Minister. He isn't exactly a saleable commodity. Who would take him in? I doubt the Americans or the British would be willing to resettle him. Not without a good deal of persuasion and some *quid pro quo* we might find difficult to provide. How would you propose we get rid of him?"

"Send him back where he came from."

Brad's astonishment must have showed on his face and in his voice.

"To the Soviet Union? You mean turn him back to the Russians?"

"That's exactly what I mean."

"But, Prime Minister, that would be tantamount to murder. I don't particularly like the man but I hardly think we should be party to his execution. The Russians would squeeze him dry and then execute him. There would be no trial."

"What his own people do to him is none of my business. I want him out of Canada. The Russians sent him here. They can take him back."

Brad started to argue but she caught him before he could open his mouth.

"Mr. Randall. I don't want any argument. The matter is closed. I want that man out of the country. That is an order."

Christ, why did he have to cross her path today? Brad drew in his breath.

"Very well, Prime Minister. I understand what you wish done but it may have to be without my involvement."

"What does that mean? Are you attempting to defy me?"

"It means, Prime Minister, that I will have to consider carefully what options are open to me in the light of your instructions about the disposal of Orion."

Brad stood up.

"Where are you going?"

"To consider those options, Prime Minister."

She stood up, pushed back her chair and walked around the

table to stand within a foot of him. She looked at him steadily.

"You do that, Mr. Randall."

She turned on her heel and, returning to her desk, began addressing herself to a pile of correspondence before her. She didn't look up as Brad let himself out of the heavy green-baize covered door.

Brad did not sleep well. Awakening at five-thirty and finding further sleep impossible, he got up quietly, being careful not to wake Marianne. He made himself coffee and retired to the study to consider the fruits of his previous night's efforts. Contemplating the discarded drafts of various letters of resignation he had attempted to write, the results were meagre. One paragraph on a single sheet of paper, and even now he was undecided whether it should start: "It is with great regret . . . . " That sounded pompous, yet it *was* with great regret. He had wrestled late into the night with various alternatives. Should he tender his resignation and declare his intention to make public his reasons? Should he simply announce his intention to take early retirement, giving some trumped-up story — ill-health or a desire for another career? At least that would avoid the brouhaha which inevitably would be associated with publicizing his real reasons for resigning, a course which was very likely to harm the Security Service. In the end, he decided upon a simple letter of resignation with a minimum of publicity as being the best course.

Sighing, he reached for a fresh sheet of paper and began to write. The telephone on the desk beside him shrilled. He grabbed for it at the first ring, hoping that the bedside phone had not wakened Marianne.

"Yes?"

"It's George. Sorry about the hour. It's about Orion."

"What about him?"

"He's dead."

"Dead? How?"

"He was found hanging by his belt in the bathroom about a half hour ago by one of the surveillance team. It looks like suicide. The Force doctor is there and has confirmed that the cause of death appears to have been strangulation. He won't be able to give a better opinion until he has performed an autopsy. I thought you would want to know immediately."

"Any chance it was murder?"

"Anything's possible, but I doubt it — we had him well-covered. I have started an investigation."

"What about Galena? Have you checked?"

"Yes, the moment I heard the news I checked with the safe house. There are two of our people there with her, one of them Corporal Susan O'Brien. Everything was normal. I told Yarborough, who's in charge, what has happened and asked him to be on the look-out for anything suspicious. I told him to order up some more men and that he could have all the additional personnel he needed. I suggested that he not tell Galena about Orion's death at this stage."

"Good. I agree she should not be told at this particular time. I think we should speed-up the plans we discussed for giving her a new identity. In the circumstances we probably should do that at once."

"Okay. I'll move on that immediately."

"Fine. Oh, George. The fewer involved in her identity change the better. I'll be over as soon as I can. I want to see the body before it's removed."

Orion's mottled face and protruding tongue was not a pleasant sight, nor was the faecal stench in the small bathroom where his body had been found hanging from overhead pipes by his heavy leather belt with the mod brass buckle. The doctor added little to what George McCain had already reported.

"There is no doubt strangulation was the cause of death. Only an autopsy will tell us if anything else contributed to it."

Brad called an emergency meeting in the "cubby-hole" — literally a post mortem. Orion's death would create a number of problems, leaving unanswered a lot of questions about the veracity of much of the information he had provided. Galena, perhaps, could fill in some of the missing pieces but large gaps would remain. Brad thought grimly that the situation was no worse than it would have been if the Prime Minister had had her way. She would have to be told of this development at once. When the meeting broke up, George McCain remained.

"George. I will have to arrange to see the Prime Minister. I have assumed that when checking on Galena's safety you also checked on Gadenus' safety?"

"I didn't do it personally, but one of my staff did. Everything is normal. I ordered the coverage on him doubled as a precaution."

"And Paul's?"

"Same story."

"Good."

* * * * * * * * * * * * * * * * * *

"Good morning, Mr. Randall. I assume you have come to tell me the results of your consideration of the 'options' available to you, as I think you phrased it yesterday?"

She smiled as she spoke which, Brad reflected, was an improvement over yesterday. Brad thought he even detected a note of cordiality in her voice.

"Well, Prime Minister, whatever may have been the outcome of my deliberations, they have been overtaken by events."

"Overtaken by what events?"

"I was informed early this morning that Orion is dead."

"Dead? How?"

"He was found hanging by his belt from the overhead pipes in the bathroom of the apartment set aside for his use in RCMP headquarters. The doctor has stated that death certainly was due to strangulation. He will not know whether there were other contributing factors until an autopsy has been performed."

"You think he may have been murdered?"

"We don't know, Prime Minister. At the moment it appears to have been suicide. A full investigation has been ordered."

"Do you think he could have been murdered?"

"I don't know, Prime Minister."

"Well, Mr. Randall. Sometimes things have a way of working themselves out. Whatever the cause of Orion's death, I can only regard it as fortuitous — fortuitous for both of us. I assume you will continue to keep me informed if you consider there are developments I should know about."

She smiled and held out her hand, a rare and uncharacteristic gesture of amity. They shook hands at the door of her office, which she held open for him.

Twelve

John Merrivale, head of the Special Analysis Group, put down his pen and pushed back his chair. He removed his glasses and rubbed his eyes. He was tired. He glanced at the clock on the wall above his desk; six-forty p.m. Outside it was dark. A light snow was falling, the odd flakes hitting the windows, their crystalline forms quickly dissolving in the radiant heat thrown off the glass. He had better telephone to say he would be late.

"Diana. I'll be a bit late. I have some work to finish. It will mean about another half hour. Sorry, but you know how it is."

Diana sighed as she replaced the receiver of the telephone. Yes, she knew "how it is". How it had been for their entire married life. When one married a man in the Security Service one also married the organization.

John Merrivale started to re-read the draft memorandum on which he was working.

Internal Memorandum

Security Classification:
Top Secret
Distribution:
Orion Indoctrinated Only
From: Special Analysis Group (Merrivale)
To: Director General
Subject: Orion
You asked the SAG, as a matter of urgency, to provide you with a preliminary assessment of the Orion case.
There are a number of serious gaps in our knowledge. Some of these we may be able to fill with additional information from the British, the Americans and others. Further discussion with Galena Nadya Gribanov (Opal) may help to fill others. Because of Orion's sudden death, however, much will remain unknown — unless, of course, the KGB were willing to help us! There also are important related questions to which we do not have the answer and likely never will.
We do not know whether the man the Americans code-named Firefly died accidentally or whether he was

murdered. Nor can we be absolutely certain that Orion's
death was due to suicide, although the available facts
strongly suggest it was. For example, we do not know what
happened between nine p.m. the night before he died, when
he was taken to his room following his confrontation with
Opal and six a.m. the following morning when his body was
found by Corporal Matthews, one of the surveillance team
assigned to guard him.

The video tapes show him preparing for sleep and show
nothing after he doused the lights at eleven minutes after
ten. The infra-red records show that he was in his rooms
for the remainder of the time. The alarms on the windows
and the door were not triggered. The audio tapes do not
reveal any unusual sound in the rooms. Since the
bathroom was not wired, it is understandable that the
sounds he would make as he died by strangulation would
not be heard through the bathroom door, which was tightly
shut when he was discovered. The logical conclusion is that
he committed suicide. However, given who he was and the
fact that we cannot state with certainty what may have
happened, SAG would argue that the possibility that he was
murdered cannot be entirely excluded.

It is useful to consider what we know and what we do not
know, in that order.

What we know:

a) That Orion's principal mission probably was to
misinform us and, through us, our allies and friends. Orion
claimed this to be the case and Opal's information appears
to corroborate it;

b) That a principal motive behind Orion's willingness to
take on the mission, entailing, as it did, his disfigurement,
was the KGB's threat that if he did not co-operate they
would use his seventeen-year-old daughter as a "swallow",
catering to the sexual appetites of Third World targets in
Moscow (diplomats and visiting VIPs);

c) That Péter Gadenus was a KGB agent;

d) That Firefly was a KGB agent in the U.S. National
Security Agency;

e) That one of the principal objectives of the KGB's
disinformation operation was to throw suspicion on senior
officials in Canada and elsewhere, e.g. Hugh Portland in
External Affairs.

What we do not know:

a) Whether there were other more important motives
behind the KGB's elaborate disinformation operation. Was
their attempt to throw suspicion onto a senior External

Affairs officer also an attempt to deflect our attention from what the KGB might regard as more important targets, e.g. someone strategically placed in the Security Service?

b) Whether Orion committed suicide or was murdered. If the latter, then how, who did it and to what purpose?

c) Whether Firefly's death was accidental or contrived. If the latter, then how, who did it and why?

d) What portions of Orion's testimony were false and to what end?

e) When Orion identified as a spy an unmarried, English-speaking officer in External Affairs, who had served as second Secretary at the Canadian embassy in Moscow in the 1960s, and now as a senior official in Ottawa, he virtually identified Portland. Why did the KGB select Portland, apart from the obvious reason that he recently was appointed a Deputy Under Secretary? Could it have been because he rebuffed a crude attempt to blackmail him while he was in Moscow and immediately told the Canadian authorities of the attempt? It would not be the first time they have sought to punish somebody for exposing their recruitment attempts;

f) Whether Department A (dezinformstsiya) of the 1st Chief Directorate was solely responsible for Orion's mission. Opal's information suggests the 1st Department of the same Chief Directorate (United States and Canada) also was involved;

g) Why was the KGB prepared to sacrifice two such apparently valuable agents as Gadenus (Stallion) and Firefly? Was this done solely for the purpose of convincing us that Orion was a genuine defector? If so, was the apparent objective, throwing suspicion on Portland, sufficiently important to warrant the sacrifice? If not, was there some other more important hidden objective(s) — see a) above?

* * * * * * * * * * * * * * * * * * *

Snow was falling heavily in Moscow, the darkened streets all but deserted. Many of the windows in the modern buildings housing the headquarters of the KGB on the outskirts of the city were still lit. A large black Ziss limousine emerged from a ramp leading to an underground garage. It turned onto the highway and disappeared into the darkness, travelling swiftly in a south-easterly direction. The man in the back seat placed the black leather briefcase he was carrying onto the heavy plush of the seat beside him and settled into the corner. The rythmic sound of the tires on the snow-covered road surface had a hypnotic effect. He slept fitfully until the car slowed down to turn right on a narrower road flanked by enormous stands of pine and birch. Soon the headlights picked out a metal barrier from which was suspended a narrow red and white striped board. To the left was a grey-painted sentry box. The guard with his automatic rifle unslung examined the driver's credentials with a small flashlight. He raised the barrier and waved them through. The dacha of the Chairman of the KGB never went unguarded. The occupant of the car reflected he might aspire to the position but that it was for ever out of his reach. Even if he had the right Party connections he was too old, and a Georgian to boot. Never mind there were worse jobs than being the head of the First Chief Directorate.

"Welcome, Comrade. Snow. I love snow. It heightens one's appreciation of everything — women, a log fire, vodka. That is the strength of Russia. Snow. Look what it did to Napoleon and Hitler."

The speaker did not impress one at first glance. Certainly he did not on casual meeting strike one as the kind of man to head the most powerful organization in the USSR. About 182 centimetres tall, with a narrow, bald head, piercing blue eyes covered by thick-lensed glasses, he had a scholarly, almost gentle manner. This benign air was belied by his voice which had a sharp, coarse cadence. This evening he wore a neatly tailored grey hunting jacket with dark green piping, and a matching pair of trousers.

"Good evening, Comrade. What you say about our weather is true. Especially about heightening one's appreciation of vodka. I admit to a thirst."

"Good. Let us drink. Over here by the fire."

The host motioned towards the large fireplace in which were several enormous logs throwing off a welcome heat. Two comfortable chairs were set back from the fire. Between them was a low table on which were set a large bottle of vodka buried in a bucket of crushed ice, an outsize bowl of Beluga caviar and a platter of black peasant bread spread with butter.

"They say the lion is the king of beasts. Perhaps, but I think the white sturgeon which inhabits our Caspian and Black Seas is at least as noble. Who ever heard of a lion giving caviar? Here, help yourself Sergei Alekseevich."

The host splashed ice-cold vodka into a couple of cut glass tumblers.

"To us, Sergei Alekseevich."

"Aaaah. That's good, Comrade."

"Yes. What is this report about Igor Petr Molodny being dead?

What does that do to Operation Cobweb?"

"He is dead. Suicide."

"Suicide? Are you sure?"

"Yes. The source is reliable. He hanged himself."

"Why?"

"We don't know. We do know it was not long after he had seen Galena Nadya Gribanov."

"Gribanov? Why the hell didn't her father give her decent Russian names? What has she to do with his death?"

"We don't know. Probably nothing. As to Operation Cobweb, it is to all intents and purposes dead also. Dead that is from the standpoint of being able to spin more web in which to entangle our enemies. At least the Americans and the Canadians are still entangled in those parts of the web which Molodny was able to spin before he killed himself. It will take them some time to disentangle themselves. However, we paid a heavy price."

"How heavy?"

"Molodny dead. The Hungarian, Gadenus — the one we nicknamed Stallion — blown. The man known to us as Jan — the one in the American National Security Agency who became a heroin addict. He was becoming too expensive and unreliable. We agreed to sacrifice him. He is dead also."

"Dead?"

"Yes. He began to talk too much."

The host poured some more vodka and helped himself to a generous spoonful of caviar.

"I see. There have been casualties. What about Gribanov?"

"Ah, Gribanov. She is a sly one. She managed to give us the slip. We still don't know exactly how. In Budapest. She was familiar with all our rabbit runs into Yugoslavia, Austria and West Germany or at least easily could have acquired the knowledge. After all, we have sent thousands of agents down those paths in recent years and she has been involved in many of those operations. She showed up briefly in Venice. But before we could take executive action, she vanished again."

Sergei Alekseevich used a spoon to spread caviar on a piece of the black bread. After finishing off the morsel in a couple of bites he continued.

"Yes, it is unfortunate. There seems little doubt that she has defected. We have confirmation she made her way to Canada. That is where her son is. We learned, some time after the event, that her son, who was assigned to the mission involving the MS *Nefertiti,* somehow survived the sinking of the ship in Canadian waters. The sinking was reported at the time in the Canadian press. We never have been able to trace him. We assume he was given a new identity by the Canadian police."

"How much did she know about Operation Cobweb?"

"Not much. When we were arranging Molodny's 'defection' we used Gribanov to place him directly in touch with the head of the Canadian security police. When Gribanov was 'debriefed' after her 'illegal' assignment in Canada, she told us her appointment as Secretary to the Canadian Politburo dealing with Security and Intelligence matters required her to be given a new security clearance. This entailed her being interviewed by the security police. The man who interviewed her, Randall, now is head of their security police."

Sergei Alekseevich paused to drink his vodka.

"To lend credulity to Molodny's contact with the Canadian security police it was agreed that Gribanov might send her son a message which would satisfy him that it was genuine."

"Was that Gribanov's suggestion?"

"I believe so."

"How was it done?"

"She sent him a short typed message. We approved the text. It merely transmitted her love. The message was affixed to a family heirloom which her son would immediately recognize."

"An ikon?"

"No. A metal egg."

"An egg?"

"Yes. Something that had been in the Gribanov family for generations. The laboratory technicians said it was a valuable and genuine piece of art from Tsarist times."

"You are sure that Gribanov did not know much about Operation Cobweb?"

"Well, she had to know it was a disinformation operation. We explained why Molodny was being sent to Canada, but not what we expected to accomplish."

"What is the assessment about the damage she can do in other fields?"

Sergei Alekseevich held out his glass. His host looked at him.

"Help yourself."

"Alas, Galena Nadya Gribanov, if she wished, could do us a great deal of damage. Her responsibilities have been varied in recent years. She is knowledgeable about much at headquarters and abroad."

"What steps are being taken to prevent her from causing us harm?"

"The difficulty is that although we think she is in Canada, we do not know where. The country is vast. Moreover, her true identity will be disguised and she will be protected."

Sergei Alekseevich took another drink of vodka.

"What steps had you in mind?"

"Her elimination, of course."

Sergei Alekseevich finished the rest of the vodka remaining in his glass.

"I . . . "

"You said something?"

"Yes, well . . . "

"Well what?"

"Her father, Anatoli Ivanovich."

"What about him? He is dead."

"I know he is dead. But when he was alive he did much for Mother Russia. We were comrades together in the early days."

"That was a long time ago Sergei Alekseevich. What has that to do with what we were talking about?"

"Nothing, I suppose. Still . . . "

"Still what, Sergei Alekseevich?"

The older man sat back in his chair, the pupils of his faded blue eyes dilated. His face was flushed. Small grains of Beluga caviar clung to one corner of his mouth. He smiled foolishly, looking at the empty bottle.

"The vodka is finished."

His host leaned forward and pressed a button on the table beside him.

"Yes, Sergei Alekseevich, and so are you. Take him away,"

The command was given to the two armed guards who suddenly appeared on either side of Sergei Alekseevich's chair.

"But Comrade . . . "

"Take him to Lubyanka. Troiksky will deal with him."

Thirteen

The Blue Line taxi stopped at the curb on Sussex Drive opposite the French Embassy. The outsize tri-colour hung motionless on the tall flagstaff in the still air of early morning. Brad Randall paid the driver. He glanced at his watch; seven fifty-two. He had eight minutes before he was due at 24 Sussex Drive, the Prime Minister's residence. The invitation to join the Prime Minister for breakfast was extended to him through the Secretary to the Cabinet the previous evening. Brad had taken the request as a command. He knew why she wished to see him and he welcomed the chance to speak to her privately.

As Brad was admitted to 24 Sussex by a maid he was surprised to find the Prime Minister standing in the hallway.

"I'm glad you were able to come. I apologize for the early hour but there is no other time on my schedule today when we can have an undisturbed discussion."

She motioned him to follow her up the graceful curved staircase to the second floor. She ushered him into a large, comfortable room on the right off the landing. Brad looked around with curiosity. He had only been on the second floor on one other occasion and that at night. He followed the Prime Minister across the room to a table set in a window embrasure overlooking the Ottawa river a hundred feet below the cliff on which the house stood. A magnificent view with the Gatineau hills providing a dramatic backdrop. On a narrow sideboard near the table were set out various fruit juices, cereals, a heated tray with two covered silver entrée dishes, from which tantalizing smells arose, a coffee urn and a toaster with a choice of sliced breads beside it.

"Please help yourself. This way we will not be interrupted. I will come directly to the point since we do not have much time. I have Cabinet at nine-thirty. I was surprised to learn from the Secretary to the Cabinet that you have submitted your resignation. I understand you wish to leave government service entirely and that you would like to do so immediately?"

"Yes. I gave the Secretary to the Cabinet my resignation in

writing to take effect as soon as it can be conveniently arranged."

"Your decision is irrevocable?"

"Yes."

"Your letter says that your reasons are entirely personal."

"Yes. That's what it says."

"Brad — I hope you don't mind me calling you by your first name — we have known each other for a long time?"

Brad did not mind but he was surprised by the uncharacteristic display of familiarity. His astonishment showed. Seeing the expression on his face the Prime Minister burst into laughter.

"I know I must appear quite formidable at times, but really I'm quite human. I want you to know I will place no obstacles in your way. But I also want you to know that I very much regret your decision — and not only because it may cause me some political difficulty."

"That is kind of you to say, Prime Minister."

"Brad, I have no desire to pry into your personal affairs. However, if there is anything I can do personally to cause you to reconsider you have but to say so."

Brad spent an inordinate amount of time buttering a piece of toast before replying. He sighed and looked directly at the Prime Minister.

"Thank you. I should have known that you would be unlikely to accept the reason I gave for resigning at face value. There are personal, very personal reasons for my decision. However, there are also other reasons which you are entitled to know about. Indeed, if you had not arranged this meeting I intended asking for an opportunity to meet with you before leaving office."

He paused to sip his coffee.

"May I speak frankly?"

"I expect nothing less from you."

"It may hurt."

"I'm a big girl."

"Well, there are three reasons for my decision to quit at this time. First, there is something for which you are responsible; second, there is some disturbing information which I received from Galena Nadya Gribanov; third, there is the state of Galena's health."

"Something I did? What?"

The Prime Minister's puzzlement was unfeigned.

"I have to be blunt."

"I've told you, I'm a big girl. Go ahead."

The laughter had gone from her voice.

"It has to do with your attitude towards Orion. You may recall my strong objection to your instructions that he be turned back to the Russians."

Her surprise was patent.

"But that question is settled. Orion is dead. You can't be serious?"

"Orion is dead but the principle implicit in your instruction to turn him back to the Soviet Union while he was alive is far from dead. You decided, purely for domestic political reasons, to sacrifice a defector; to commit him to certain death. Orion was a most unattractive specimen who deliberately attempted to mislead us, and very nearly succeeded. However, he was in our custody. We were responsible for his safety and well-being. To have been prepared to condemn him to death simply because his continued presence might be politically embarrassing is something I find unacceptable. It is the kind of approach which the KGB would take. It is not one that we should take.

Espionage is a dirty business and sometimes the measures which have to be taken to deal with it effectively are not in accordance with the Marquis of Queensberry rules. However, there are certain rules, certain principles, which must be observed if we are to avoid no more than carbon copies of our opponents. In my book the abandonment of our responsibility for the safety of a defector to satisfy some domestic political concern falls in that category. On top of that, in professional terms, it would have been a stupid action. In no time word would have filtered down the mysterious grapevine of spies and counter-spies that Canada could no longer be trusted to honour its commitments to defectors."

The Prime Minister sat staring at Brad, speechless. He waited, but she said nothing. He continued.

"My second reason for quitting is that Galena Nadya has confirmed the suspicion, which already had formed in my mind even before Orion's death, that the Security Service itself may have been penetrated by the KGB. Without being able to identify anyone Galena Nadya has told me she saw material in Moscow strongly suggesting there is a traitor in the Security Service. The kind of material she mentioned could only have come from the top of the Security Service — from one of a very limited number of senior officers. Logically, I would be among the suspects along with some of my most trusted advisers such as George McCain and John Merrivale. I have worked too closely with these men to be able to investigate them properly and impartially. By resigning I have done two things for you. I have eliminated myself as a suspect, assuming, of course, that the leaks will continue after my departure. I have also made it possible for you to appoint someone from the outside who is capable of plugging the leak. If you wish I will be happy to assist you in selecting my successor. It has to be someone from outside the Service."

Brad paused. The Prime Minister merely looked at him, apparently still at a loss for words.

"My third reason for resigning is entirely personal. I wish to marry Galena Nadya. Clearly I could not do so while remaining as head of the Security Service."

"A short time ago Galena learned from her doctors that she has a form of bone cancer which cannot be cured. She is dying. The doctors doubt she has much more than a year to live."

He poured himself some more coffee to cover the difficulty he was having in speaking. He swallowed a sip of the scalding liquid before continuing.

"While Galena Nadya was living out a normal life span I was able to sublimate my love for her — pretend it wasn't there. I can't do that any more. I want to spend as much time as I can with her before she dies. I want to be with her, to love her and if possible to comfort her. Probably it is she who will comfort me."

He brushed the corner of his eye and smiled. It was not a forced smile.

"That's about it, Prime Minister."

"This may sound strange, Brad, but I think Galena Nadya Gribanov is a lucky woman."

The Prime Minister pushed back her chair from the table. She smoothed her skirt as she walked to the window. There was a long silence before she turned to speak to him. He didn't interrupt her as she spoke.

"Thank you for being so frank. Too many people try to tell me only what they think I want to hear. You have never been guilty of that. You are probably incapable of doing so, which is why I shall miss you. If it were not for what you have told me of your personal reasons for leaving I would do everything in my power to persuade you to change your mind.

"I will want to be briefed in more detail about the possible leak in the Security Service. That is very disturbing information. I may need your help, despite your protestations. I have to put my trust someplace and as far as I am concerned you are completely above suspicion.

"So far as the Orion affair is concerned, I am afraid we shall have to agree to disagree. Clearly we approach the matter from quite different perspectives. I have responsibilities as Prime Minister and as leader of the Party. It is not always possible to keep them separate. I do my best — just as you have done your best in your quite different responsibilities as head of a rather unusual agency of government.

"The possibility that the Security Service has been penetrated by the KGB makes the question of your replacement of crucial importance. I appreciate your offer to help. Who do you suggest?"

"The choice is limited but I think the most likely candidate already is known to you. He is in the Privy Council Office, handling the Security and Intelligence secretariat."

"You mean Hannibal?"

"Yes. Steve Hannibal."

"But he is so young."

"True, but in this job that can be an advantage. However, in Hannibal's case he has managed to pack in an astonishing amount of experience which will stand him in good stead. He served in External on the security and intelligence side, making many useful contacts in the international community. He had a stint in the National Defence College in Kingston and, until his present job in the PCO, he acted as an adviser to the Immigration department on the security aspects of immigration policy. He is fluently bilingual. Indeed, I believe he is trilingual, since in addition to French and English he also speaks Arabic."

"Thank you for the suggestion. I'll have a word with the Secretary to the Cabinet."

She glanced at her wrist watch and rose. She held out her hand.

"I'm sorry, Brad, I must go. Thank you again for not being afraid to speak your mind. I think your decision to marry Galena Nadya is the right one to have taken. I may not make it to the wedding but I shall be thinking of you both."

The Prime Minister led him towards the landing. Brad followed. As he made his way down the staircase he sensed a movement at the head of the stairs and turned to see the Prime Minister watching his descent. As she caught his glance she raised her hand and waved.

"Good bye, Brad Randall. Bless you."